D1358162

Also by Gail Godwin

NOVELS

Evensong

The Good Husband

Father Melancholy's Daughter

A Southern Family

The Finishing School

A Mother and Two Daughters

Violet Clay

The Odd Woman

Glass People

The Perfectionists

SHORT STORIES

Dream Children

Mr. Bedford and the Muses

NONFICTION

Heart: A Natural History of the Heart-Filled Life

BALLANTINE BOOKS NEW YORK

Evenings at Five

A NOVEL AND FIVE STORIES

Gail Godwin

With illustrations by Frances Halsband

For
Robert Starer

Vienna, Austria, January 8, 1924–
Woodstock, New York, April 22, 2001

Contents

Introduction

My Christina stories were inaugurated in 1999, when the editor of *Brightleaf: New Writing from the South* asked me if I had a story for a planned special issue on formative religious experiences. I didn't, but I said I would write one for him. Having a specific assignment always stimulates me. I wrote "Possible Sins," which begins with eleven-year-old Christina's dialogue with her priest in the confessional and evolves into a life-long friendship, ending with their discussion over lunch, many years later, of possible ways they might get in touch after one of them dies.

Not long after, an editor invited me to contribute to a coffee-table book of Christmas stories. Each story had to fit on a single page

across from the glossy illustration to accompany
its text. So I wrote a very short story, "Largesse,"
narrated in first person. When the book project
fell through, I decided to expand my mini-story
into the longer form I luxuriate in: an almost-
novella length. I changed the narration to third
person, and, realizing that the material had the
same autobiographical underpinnings as "Possible Sins," I named the protagonist Christina
again. She's fifteen years old now and goes to
spend Christmas with her rich Texas relatives,
where she finds herself both awed and repelled
by the opulence they lavish on her.

I think it was when I was putting the finishing
touches on "Largesse" that I began to envision a
whole range of Christina stories that could cruise
back and forth through time and pounce on the
hot spots, those places in Christina's journey that
mark a turning point for her, or test her strength
and character, stories that might eventually add
up to a fictional autobiography, which I would
call *The Passion of Christina*.

Somewhat later on, I decided to include certain stories or memoirs in which the first-person narrator shared Christina's personal history. Thus the story "Old Lovegood Girls," whose narrator is known only as "I," and the memoir pieces "Mother and Daughter Ghosts" and "Waltzing with the Black Crayon" are part of Christina's/ Gail's ongoing chronicle. Each recounts a crucial turning point: Christina finds, then loses, her father; Christina goes on a last journey with her mother; Christina meets a mentor whose quirky, gentle tactics finally succeed in dragging her across the line between wanting (and equally fearing) to become a writer and simply being one.

And then, in the early spring of 2002, as the first anniversary of Robert Starer's death approached, I was sitting on the sofa with my five o'clock drink and looking at his empty chair across from me. And I began jotting down a list of all the sounds I remembered from our former cocktail hour: the ice machine making more ice, the cat's toenails clicking on the floor, the sound of a jet gaining altitude after its takeoff from Albany, and, of course, the sound of Robert's deep, rumbly voice announcing that "the Pope has just called," which meant it was time for our happy hour. First came the cataloging of sounds and then came the opening lines:

> Five o'clock sharp. *"Ponctualité est la politesse des rois"*: Rudy quoting his late father, a factory owner (textiles) in Vienna before the Nazis came. The Pope's phone call, followed by the grinding of the ice, a growling, workmanlike sound, a lot like Rudy's own sound. . . . He built Christina's drink with loving precision. . . .

Why, I've been asked, did you feel you had to write *Evenings at Five* as fiction? Why not just write it as a memoir?

I never considered the memoir form because I wanted to write a tale. The major experience was real—all too real—but I needed to reserve the right to add and subtract and embellish, to "make it up" when my instincts tugged me in that direction. After decades of writing fiction I have learned that in the middle of "inventing," the most amazing discoveries jump out at you: surprises of memory and feeling that shed new light on the literal happenings. So it was "Rudy" and "Christina" from the beginning; I even changed the name of the cat.

As I said, I knew I wanted to write a tale. But what I didn't know until I got deeper into *Evenings at Five* (whose working title was "The Pope Called") was that I was writing a ghost story. An encounter with a real absence can lead to a sounding through of certain values and energies of the absent person, qualities that transcend death. *Evenings* is dominated by a man's values, eccentricities, and creative energies. The vibrato of his personality comes pulsing through the space he once inhabited, and in the pregnant silence his partner listens to him more closely than ever. The word *person* itself comes down to us from the Latin *per-sonāre,* which means "to sound through."

In that sense, I now realize, all the Christina stories collected here could qualify as ghost stories.

Evenings at Five

Rudy's chair

Chapter One

Five o'clock sharp. *"Ponctualité est la politesse des rois"*: Rudy quoting his late father, a factory owner (textiles) in Vienna before the Nazis came. The Pope's phone call, followed by the grinding of the ice, a growling, workmanlike sound, a lot like Rudy's own sound, compliments of the GE model Rudy had picked out fourteen years ago when they built this house. *Gr-runnch, gr-runnch, grr-rr-runnch.* ("And look! It even has this tray you pull down to mix the drinks." Rudy retained the enthusiasms of childhood.) He built Christina's drink with loving precision after the Pope's call. Rudy did the high Polish voice, overlaid with an Italian accent: "Thees is John Paul. My cheeldren, eet is cocktail time."

Or sometimes Christina's study phone would not ring. Rudy simply emerged from his studio below and called brusquely up to her in his basso profundo: "Hello? The Pope just called. Are you ready for a drink?"

The ominous rolled *r*'s on the "ready" and "drink": if you're not, you'd better be. I won't be here forever, you know.

The cavalier slosh of Bombay Sapphire (Rudy never measured) over the ice shards. The *fssst* as he loosened the seltzer cap and added the self-respecting splash that made her able to call it a gin and soda. Then, marching over to the sink: "I need Ralph." Ralph was their best serrated knife. The thinly cut slice of lime oozed fresh juice. Rudy cut well; he cut his own music paper, and he had been cutting Christina's hair exactly as she liked it for twenty-eight years. And in summer, a sprig of mint from the garden, a hairy, pungent variety given to them by the wife of a pianist who had recorded Rudy's music. Sometimes Rudy joined Christina in the gin and soda. Her financial man from Buffalo had given them two twelve-ounce tumblers with old-fashioned ticker tapes etched into the surfaces. She always kept them in the freezer, so they would frost up as soon as they hit the air.

Other times Rudy would say, "I need a Scotch tonight." That went into a different glass, a lovely cordial shape etched with grapes, given to him by the daughter of a pasha who had invited him to her houseboat parties in Cairo back in '42 and called him Harpo because his assignment in the Royal Air Force had been playing piano and harp to keep up troop morale. "I need a Scotch tonight" could mean either that his work had gone extremely well or that some unwelcome aspect of reality (his music publisher sending back sloppily edited orchestra parts, being put on hold by his health insurance provider, being put on hold by anyone at all) had undermined his creative momentum.

"Thees is Il Papa calling from the Vatican. Cheeldren, eet is cocktail time."

Christina was a cradle Episcopalian who had gone to a Catholic school run by a French order of nuns in North Carolina. Rudy was a nonpracticing Jew who had gone to a Catholic *Gymnasium* in Vienna until age fourteen, when the Nazis came. Rudy always liked to tell how there were two Jews and one Protestant in his class at the *Gymnasium,* "and the Protestant had the worst of it by far." So Rudy and Christina shared an affectionate fascination with Popes, especially this one, with his hulking masculine shoulders before they began to stoop, and his nonstop traveling, and all the languages.

What did I think, that we had forever? Christina asked herself, sipping the gin and soda she now made for herself. Often Rudy had interrupted himself in midsentence to explode at her: "You're *not* listening!"

What was *I listening to? The ups and downs of*

my own day's momentum. We were both "ah-tists,"
as the real estate lady who sold us our first house pro-
nounced it. She herself had been married to an ah-tist.
Her husband's novel had been runner-up for the
Pulitzer, she told us, the year Anthony Adverse *won.*
Her name was Odette, as in Swann's downfall. Rudy
was fifty-two and I was thirty-nine and neither of us
knew, until Odette carefully explained it to us, that
you could buy a house without having all the money
to pay for it up front.

Christina would arrange herself on the black
leather sofa they had splurged on in their midlife
prosperity (a combined windfall of a bequest
from Rudy's late uncle in Lugano, with whom
Rudy had played chess, and a lucrative two-
book contract for Christina, in those bygone
days when there were enough competing pub-
lishers to run up the auction bid) and which the
Siamese cats had ruined within six months. She
would cross her ankles on the Turkish cushions
on top of the burled-wood coffee table and train
her myopic gaze on Rudy's long craggy face and
familiar form reassuringly present in his Stickley

Christina's desk with ragged thesaurus
and Rudy's metronome

armchair on the other side of the fireplace. An editor had once told Rudy he looked like "a happy Beckett." Christina felt rich in her bounty: the workday was over and she had this powerful companion pulsing his attention at her, and her whole drink to go. They raised their cocktail glasses to each other.

"So what did you do today?" She usually jumped in first, knowing he would tend to her novelist's gripes or breakthroughs later.

"I finished the next movement of my piano sonata. If you like, I'll play it for you later. Oh, and I had a call from Henning. He wants to conduct the choral version of *Night Thoughts* in Boston."

"I didn't know you had a choral version of *Night Thoughts*."

"That's because you *don't listen to me*."

"That's not a fair statement. It's just that I can't keep track of all your works—"

"I keep track of yours."

"Yeah, well, I only have ten novels and two story collections. You have *hundreds* of pieces.

Please don't ruin our evening. Tell me about Henning. That's wonderful he wants to do it in Boston."

"Yes. Maybe we'll go if I'm still here."

Rudy blew up quickly, but he blew over almost as quickly. Christina marinated her resentments, then simmered them over a low flame for days.

At other cocktail hours they would sit facing each other in silence on either side of the fireplace. (Two yards apart between his knees and hers: Christina had measured the distance after his death when she was wandering around taking inventories of all she missed about him.) They would sip their drinks and she would sigh and he would brood at her from under his eyebrows, until one of them asked: "What are you thinking?"

"I was thinking about my new book," she might say. "It's no good. I think it's died on me." And that might get them going for a whole evening, through a refill and then a bottle of wine with dinner, after which he would offer to read what she had so far. And she would creep upstairs and lie still in their bed and wait for his heavy tread on the stairs, and his shaggy head appearing round the door to say something like: "It's magnificent, it's going to be your best yet. But you've got to give Margaret a boyfriend—this is the twentieth century and she's twenty-one years old."

Or: "What are you thinking?" she would ask, breaking the silence first. Sometimes Rudy exploded with a tirade against toneless composers or a particular enemy. But most often he would look pensive and a little superior, as if he'd been called back from a place she couldn't go.

"I wasn't thinking. I was hearing music."

Freezer with gin reserves and ticker-tape glass

Chapter Two

⬥⬥⬥

The gin was flavored with not the usual one or two botanicals, but *ten*. Almonds and lemon peel, from Spain; licorice, from China; juniper berries and orris root, from Italy; angelica root, from Saxony; coriander seeds, from Morocco; cassia bark, from Indochina; cubeb berries, from Java; grains of paradise, from West Africa. International, like Rudy himself. Five nationalities, but he refused to claim the German one ("That was forced on us when Austria was invaded"). A gifted linguist, he spoke fluent German, Hebrew, English, Italian ("When I had my Fulbright, I wanted to see if I could learn a new language after forty; my teacher was pretty, she lived on the Piazza Mattei, across from the Fountain of Turtles"). He could get by socially in French when they traveled, and could erupt with impressive spurts of Russian and Arabic should the occasion arise.

He spoke a precise English, slightly British from his years in the Royal Air Force in Palestine. His foreign accent was not in the pronunciation of words but in his ornamental phrasings: even his recorded phone message danced with Rudy-ish melisma. He had a Shakespearean range of vocabulary and a richer command of American slang than Christina did. When a new situation called for it, he cobbled his own words: "the doctor removed two cancerettes from my face," "Christina, you are turning into a curmudgeoness." His after-lunch nap was his "tryst with Morphia," who dyed her hair a straw blond and drove up each day from New Jersey. His

tempo markings ("creepily," "dreamily," "elegantly," "quite brittle," "exploring," "lackadaisi-
cal," "amorous," "relaxed with a bounce") were
drolly precise.

He loved spoonerisms and his were top
quality, often resonating with prophetic after-
tones. His favorite, "The Cope palled," was a
prime example. When the Pope stopped calling
every evening at five, Christina's religious life
took a turn for the worse. She no longer found
assurance in the familiar churchly trappings.
None of them provided compensation or expla-
nation for what she had lost.

The Cope indeed had palled.

She and Rudy had started their life together
in a two-hundred-year-old rented farmhouse in
an upstate New York village chartered by Queen
Anne. They sat in two orange plastic lawn chairs
in the living room and put their glasses and the
bottle of sherry on the deep window seat between them, until their ancient landlady dropped
in one evening and saw the state of things and
sent down two armchairs and a coffee table.

They drank Taylor's New York State sherry in those frugal days when they had thrown over everything but their work in order to be together: Rudy had left his ordered family life in Manhattan, and Christina had given up her tenure-track teaching job in Iowa. Rudy rented a not-very-good piano from a local dealer, and Christina typed on a shaky table found for ten dollars at a local antique store. The sherry was followed by a cheap Spanish wine at dinner. On one special occasion, Rudy dropped a bottle of Mouton-Cadet on the paved driveway of the farmhouse as he was getting out of the car. The image of his woeful face (childlike in its despair) as he surveyed the smashed bottle was graven on Christina's heart.

Now that Rudy was dead, Christina listened to him more closely than ever. There, the same two yards away from the cat-ravaged leather sofa (one of the cats had died young from heart failure), loomed his Stickley armchair. There was the tall Turkish pillow he used for propping up his back against chest pain. Only his kingly size was missing from the picture. The long face with the high forehead and thatch of white hair floated only in the gloaming of her memory.

But now, at the ghostly cocktail hours, she hung on his every echo. No need any longer for him to growl "You aren't listening!" because Christina was. Intensely. She heard everything that decorated his silences: the oil burner kicking in, the refrigerator (making more ice), a southbound jet gaining altitude after its Albany takeoff. The click of the surviving cat's toenails on the pine floors as he made his proprietary rounds.

"You *are* listening!" Rudy might now remark. And, always curious about her inner workings, he would want to know exactly what she heard.

"I was hearing," Christina spoke aloud to the empty chair, "something you might have said yourself. But first I have to tell you what led up to it. Remember, the last evening in your hospital room, you were sitting on the side of the bed, you were feeling much better, we expected they'd drain you and refuel you like the other

17

View of below from Christina's study

times and send you home in a day or two. You'd finished your dinner, eating the whole salad with French dressing, picking at the meat sauce and leaving the pasta, drinking the black coffee and spurning the red Jell-O with Reddi-wip. You'd been telling me about a passage you liked in the Muriel Spark novel you were reading, where she says if you want to lose weight, eat and drink the same as always, only half, and then adds that this advice is included in the price of the book. 'I liked that,' you said. Then I said I thought I would skip church tomorrow and come to the hospital early, and we agreed I should get home before dark. And I stood up and kissed you and said in a jokey-flirtatious way, 'Don't you dare leave me.' And you looked at me fiercely from under your shaggy brows and rumbled, 'We still have some more time together,' and I drove home reassured.

"Though of course we didn't. Next morning, I had to be content with saying farewell to your body in the hospital bed. But here's what I was hearing just now, in this voice I sometimes hear things. It's a wiser version of my own voice, and it was saying like a mantra: 'Absent in his presence, present in his absence.'

"And then I had this further idea. That somewhere in the gulf between those opposites, 'absence and presence' or 'presence and absence,' might lie the secret of eternal life."

"Or the secret of death."

Death had always fascinated Rudy far more than eternal life. Was that a Jewish thing?

"Or maybe," Christina went on addressing the chair, "it's all one and the same, only the order of opposites is reversed: absence in presence, or presence in absence. Depending on where you are on your journey."

"Would you like a little more?"

Christina could still hear the pitch of Rudy's voice asking this. Indulgent, protective, rumbly, but with no hint of a growl. What he was asking was: shall we continue this a little longer, this soul-to-soul cocktail hour we have built for ourselves over the years?

"Just a *little,* thank you." The happy reply of drinkers all over the world.

Rudy's ghost brought her the refill.

It was winter now and the wild wind screamed around the corners of the house they had built together in this Catskill hamlet fourteen years ago. "The Villa," "The Factory," or "The Orphanage," they called it, depending on their mood. Rudy had dreamed up the first two names, and Christina had contributed the third after her mother died.

"You are with me always." Christina continued talking to the chair, lifting the icy topped-off tumbler to her lips. "As in 'Lo, I am with you, always.' A strong personality comes into the world, touches some people, infuriates others, then goes out again. The absent one remains present to those people. Just as those people had their absent moments in his presence. Of course, nobody testified to all the times the disciples were fed up or bored out of their minds with Jesus. 'Why is he making us walk so far in this heat? Who does he think he is, why does he go on and on and then yell at us for not listening, why does he have to have such a short fuse?' "

And the wind whistled down the chimney, just like in the old stories.

In somebody else's story, Christina thought, the wind would whistle down the chimney, she would look up one evening, she would focus, focus, focus on the shadows in the Stickley chair, and suddenly *he* would materialize, sitting bolt upright against his Turkish pillow to ward off chest pain. Dickens could toss off such a manifestation as easily as flipping a pancake, Henry James or Edith Wharton would finesse it with ambiguities, but this was Christina's story, and if she forced or finessed anything, she might miss the secret with her name on it.

Ralph the knife, with lime, mint, and ticker-tape glass

Chapter Three

Seven months had gone by. On the day of Rudy's April funeral some Jewish friends had given her a *yahrzeit* candle, to keep lit for the seven days of shiva. Now it was November and she took the empty red glass container with the Star of David to the local candle store and asked if it could be refilled and a new wick put in. No problem, they said.

The young rabbi who had conducted Rudy's funeral and burial with imagination and aplomb

turned out to be a Jewish mystic. She told
Christina that she would come every afternoon
at five and sit shiva with her and help with the
guests. And on the seventh evening, if Christina
so desired, the rabbi would be glad to walk
around the outside of the house with her and
help dispatch Rudy's spirit on its transmigratory
journey and then cook dinner for her. Christina
said she was not ready to dispatch Rudy's spirit
and that she thought she would like to be alone
on the seventh evening. The rabbi took it sport-
ingly and continued to show up at five each afternoon in her chic and original outfits. Trim little
tweed suits with midcalf skirts, dashing scarves
cleverly knotted, colored socks that matched her
Guatemalan pillbox hats that served as feminine
yarmulkes. She was tiny with long, slim feet,
and wore different pairs of hand-sewn Italian
lace-ups greatly admired by Christina and the
friends who came to the shiva-salons for Rudy.
The rabbi didn't proselytize, but shared her
mystical lore if asked. She was a great asset at
the five o'clock gatherings: artfully told first-

person ghost stories are always a draw, and the rabbi told them well—how she finally had persuaded her beloved great-uncle to leave her kitchen on the fifth anniversary of his death, arranged a little ceremony, then opened a window and felt his unbound spirit take off like a freed hawk into the night. The dead little girl who had to instruct her mother through a dream that it was time to let go. Plus some Kabbalistic timetables of the spirit's itinerary, how long it lingers where, especially in the first year after death.

On the seventh day after Rudy's burial, Christina had been sitting alone on the ruined leather sofa with her gin, the spring sun pouring in at the exact spot where Rudy always had to shield his face at this time of year. She kept a sharp watch over the *yahrzeit* candle. It sputtered out at 7:43, and she stumbled tipsily out into the blue-green dusk, just in case Rudy's spirit was attempting a subtle getaway to spare her the wrenching pain.

A full-grown black bear was sitting with its

back to her on the lawn. Hearing her intake of breath, it rose with magnificent insouciance and loped off into the woods with its sleek high-bottomed gait.

And now it was November, and Christina, at first a faithful and then an increasingly immoderate observer of the ghostly cocktail hour (the 1.75-liter blue bottles with Queen Victoria's brooding three-quarter profile were replaced weekly now, with sometimes a 750-milliliter junior size in reserve in case she should run short on the weekends), was hours away from a nice little health scare.

Soon it would be seven months exactly from the April day when the undertakers lowered Rudy's coffin into the grave and the mourners formed two lines and took turns shoveling earth on the plain pine box with the Star of David on top.

In the Catskill hamlet where Rudy and Christina had settled, the artists (and their families or significant others) had their own cemetery. Odette, now resting there next to her novelist husband, had told them about the "ahtists' cemetery" back in 1976 and encouraged them to buy their plots right away, as space was running out. They had procrastinated, of course, and were saved only the day of Rudy's death by a new couple from Christina's church who made her a present of their two plots.

"Gil has decided he definitely does not want to be buried next to his mother," the wife had told Christina.

Five o'clock sharp. Completely dark in November. "Punctuality is the courtesy of kings": Rudy always quoted his father's maxim in French and then translated it for her, as if she might not remember from time to time.

Secure that her full glass (lime but no mint in the winter) with the ticker tape awaited her on its cocktail napkin, Christina paced herself, lighting some candles. The *yahrzeit* one wasn't back from the store yet. She walked to and fro across the rugs, gazed up at the high ceiling, remembered how they had stood like awed children watching the great bluestone fireplace being laid, stone by stone, by masons who knew what they were doing. Neither of them quite believed they were causing a house they had imagined for themselves to come into existence in the real world. And the builder and all the workmen took care of them like children, pointing out the advantages of having the house face south-east instead of northeast, tactfully suggesting that a bathroom door open not directly into the kitchen but into the hallway just outside.

"It's splendid, but are there enough closets?" Christina's literary agent asked when the house was being framed.

"Oh, Lord, closets," said Christina. "I guess we need some more."

Their one requirement, when the builder was making sketches, was that Rudy's studio would be downstairs on the northeast side of the house and Christina's study would be upstairs on the southwest side.

"I can't stand for anyone to overhear me composing," Rudy explained to the builder. "Even when they say they don't hear."

On some level of consciousness, Christina thought, *I must have heard all those years of Rudy's compositions forming themselves phrase by phrase, probably even note by note, but I told him the truth when I said I didn't hear, that I was scrunched into some dark soundproof chamber behind my eyeballs, straining for flashes of images that then had to have words matched to them. And he believed me because he had caught me not listening so many times. But then, later, when I heard something of his played at a concert, I could re-member hearing it come into being. Sometimes I even had a visual memory of what the day had looked like outside my study window when he was downstairs in his studio plinking and plonking toward a certain sound and then suddenly bursting into a fully realized cascade of melody. And then the scrape of the piano bench, the transfer of his body (thur–rump) into his leather desk chair, followed by alternating solos of metronome and electric eraser. I heard without know-ing I was hearing all the outer sounds of a work being captured.*

She switched on the lamp, sank into the clawed leather with a sigh, crossed her ankles on

Bathroom outside kitchen

the pillows, and—still not yet reaching for the frosted glass—dipped into Rudy's 2001 At-a-Glance appointment diary, the only record of himself he kept.

This was the final one, with entries—doctors' appointments, upcoming concerts of his music, dating six months beyond his death. ("How I love being the only one on the program who still has a dash after his birth date," he always said at concerts when his music was played along with that of the classic composers.)

The other appointment diaries, dating back to 1973, the year they had moved in together, lay tumbled beside her on the sofa. Her stash of elliptic Rudy chronicles to carry her through coming nights. In earlier years, Aspen, Geneva, Tel Aviv, all their trips together, the final one being to Stockholm, and the faculty meetings, recording sessions, rehearsals, premieres, and then more and more doctors began to fill up the pages until the final ones looked like these:

10:00 Allis

2:00 Dr. Donnelly

C in NYC

10:00 Allis

11:30 Justine

3:00 Drugstore

11:00 Dr. Paolini

C in Chicago

11:00 Bud (shots)

10:00 Allis

3:30 Dr. Ladd

C in Washington

Cocktails Rosens NYET

Dr. Salzman? NYET

10:00 Allis

C home

Allis was the seventy-seven-year-old Norwegian nurse who came three times a week to give Rudy his Procrit injection and neck massage. She also stayed overnight when Christina was away on speaking engagements. Allis had spoiled the cat by letting him sleep with her and putting out a short personal glass of water for him on the night table so he wouldn't get his face caught in her tall one: a practice Christina now continued. The lovely Justine, a dancer, was Rudy's exercise therapist, although he couldn't do much, but he always came home feeling revived because he had a little crush on her. Dr. Donnelly was Rudy's oncologist and hematologist, Dr. Paolini was his kidney doctor, Dr. Ladd his cardiologist, Dr. Salzman his ophthalmologist. Bud was the surviving cat, now in his own seventies in cat years, and *nyet* ("no" in Russian) meant Rudy had canceled.

Christina leafed through the last appointment diary. Red ink was reserved for beginning or finishing a work ("Began *Job's Muses* in earnest. Finished *Epitaph for an Artist*. Finished *Insomnia*"). The only other entries inscribed in red were Rudy's transfusions or his chemo. Bone marrow biopsies and skeletal surveys got only black or blue ink. Christina herself ("C") had never rated Rudy's red ink. Ah-tists could be severe when it came to priorities. The longest of all of

Rudy's red–ink entries was in the 1997 At-a-Glance, during a week of chemo treatment for his multiple myeloma.

Positive but not exuberant
Resigned but not depressed
Finished piano quintet

Did the adjectives refer to the mood of his quintet or to his state of mind that day? Now listening to the quintet more carefully than she ever had before—his most somber, but with glimmers of pure tranquillity—Christina concluded it was probably a conjunction of both.

She sipped her drink and thought of how she had been so eager to get home before dark when Rudy only had twelve more hours left in the world. She sipped and sobbed like a child. If only she had known, she would have stayed in his room till the ICU nurses kicked her out. If only she had stayed. But she had gone home and read a novel late into the night, imagining Rudy either asleep or reading his Muriel Spark.

Back in the kitchen for a refill—Bud had emerged from somewhere and was sitting expectantly in front of his dish—she felt a rush of affinity with Queen Victoria as she cradled the heavy blue 1.75-liter bottle and studied the monarch's gloomy countenance. Well, what did the queen have to smile about? Even though she continued to have his clothes laid out every evening, her beloved Albert was dead, and she was fat from all the state dinners, and what was left?

When Christina had lived in London in her twenties, she had gotten to know the servants' chef at Buckingham Palace. He'd taken her on a grand tour of the servants' wing and introduced her to his colleagues. One of them had told her that Queen Victoria's nightly bottle of Black Label had continued to be delivered to her quarters until 1956 because no one had thought to rescind the order.

The phone rang in Rudy's studio. After four rings, his voice, which a conservatory student once described as "an octave below God's," came on.

"This is Rudolf Geber. Please leave your name and number, and your call will be returned as soon as *pos*-sible."

"As soon as *pos*-sible" took a playful leap up the scale, ornamenting the concept of what was possible with typical Rudy-ish melisma.

Christina slugged back her drink, some of it spilling down her chin.

"Damn it, Rudy, you could probably materialize in that chair if you wanted to. So could you, God. I don't know why I bother with either of you. Damn you both, my heart is broken."

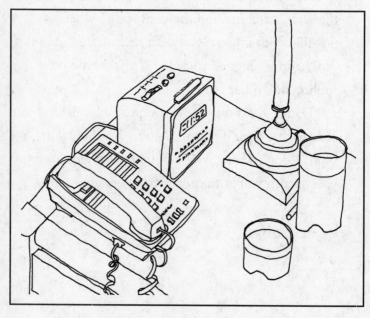

Christina's bedroom phone, with clock, cat's short glass,
and her tall glass

Chapter Four

At some point she lurched up to bed, Bud weaving in front of her as they climbed the stairs.

"Don't cross *over* like that," Christina slurred irritably. "That's the way cat owners break legs."

The night was a horror. Dry mouth. Racing heart. Nausea. Dizziness. Ugly faces leered on the insides of her eyelids. Coming attractions of her future, perhaps near future, played themselves out. Who was that old novelist who fell in the toilet when she got drunk, and her faithless young protégé spared no details in his popular memoir after her death? Christina thrashed around in what was left of the king-size space, Rudy's former half being littered with books and papers, until Bud got disgusted with rearranging himself and went downstairs in a huff. Each time she dozed off she was awakened by ringing in her ears or stabbing in her eyeballs or afterimages of flashing lights, as if someone had been taking nonstop pictures of her while she slept. For the tenth or twelfth time that night she checked the digital green numbers on the bedside clock.

Only this time there were no numbers, just a watery green blob. She sat up and turned on the lamp. Everything in the room, even the precise English landscape paintings on the wall three feet away, swam behind a thick gluey scrim. Faint with fright, she made her way to the bathroom, holding on to things. The face in the mirror was so indistinct it didn't have eyes or a mouth. She sat on the toilet, head in hands, and planned the rest of her life. Learning Braille. Having to depend on others for rides, having to pretend to be a good sport. ("The worst thing, for Christina. Why couldn't it have been her hearing? But we can't choose those things, can we? And she's taking it so well.")

She could not bring herself to call 911, though she had done it five times for Rudy. The rescue squad certainly knew their way to the house, and she knew the drill: oxygen first, then the EKG, the questions, the radioing in to the ER, Rudy's deep voice behind the mask barking orders for Christina to pack his medicines from the kitchen shelf in the Ziploc bag that would accompany him to the hospital, calling them out with his magnificently rolled *r*'s: "Toprol, Procardia, Zestril . . . " She knew most of the squad members by name and where they worked in town.

On Rudy's final trip, six of them transported him out the door sitting bolt upright on the stretcher. "You look like Pharaoh being carried forth on his litter," Christina said, making him

Christina's bed

smile behind his mask as they bore his noble
bulk to the waiting ambulance, its red lights already flashing. He told them he was feeling a little better already from the oxygen.

But now, crouched on the toilet, Christina
knew she would not be rousing the jeweler and
the IBM couple and the retired stockbroker from
their beds or be summoning the young police-
men from their night patrols. If the best of her
life was over, she preferred to postpone facing it
for a few more hours. She did go so far as to
drag herself over to the sink and swallow an as-
pirin, remembering the TV commercial of the
man collapsing on the tennis court and his son
whipping out a Bayer. Then she felt her way
back to bed and lay down and closed her eyes
and breathed in and out, using the *ujjāyī* breath
her yoga instructor had taught her.

By morning her sight was normal, and she
went to church. Though the Cope had palled
since Rudy's death, she continued to go because
church was something she had grown up knowing how to do. And she looked forward to

Father Paul's extemporaneous sermons. Startling things sometimes came out of his mouth as he stood in the aisle in his alb and chasuble with no notes: "we just have to accept our inseparability from God" had been a recent one. Also the parishioners at St. Aidan's comprised the bulk of her social life. Important human dramas were in progress there: the retired sea captain who was losing his memory, the little boy fighting cancer, the lovely young teacher who had been proposed to by two men on the same day. Also, Christina liked to dress up, and today was her Sunday to read the epistle.

After church, the Mallows, the couple who had given Christina and Rudy their plots at the artists' cemetery, invited her to brunch and were so solicitous of her that she burst into tears and confided she might be going blind. They insisted on driving her to the emergency room. Gilbert told her about the time last summer he had been reading the paper and all of a sudden there were little colored explosions on the page. He drove himself to a specialist, who steadied his head in an apparatus and while telling him the plot of a novel flashed something at Gilbert's eye. "There, all fixed," the specialist said, having lasered together a retinal fissure. If necessary, the Mallows would be glad to drive Christina to the same specialist, even make the appointment for her. They remained with her in the ER all afternoon while she underwent tests. A CT scan ruled out a brain tumor. The doctor on duty guessed she had suffered a migraine and wrote her a prescription in case she felt another coming on. By then it was time for dinner and the Mallows took her to a fish restaurant by the river. Christina thanked them profusely all the way home.

"Oh, it was fun hanging out with you," Eve Mallow said.

Gilbert added, "When Rudy was alive, you two barricaded yourselves, which was understandable, with all his health problems. You were both formidable, though you seemed the more accessible of the two."

The idea of sharing Rudy's formidability did not displease Christina at all.

Rudy's medicine shelf

Chapter Five

*C*hristina's primary-care physician, Dr. Gray, sent her immediately to an eye doctor, young and thorough, who ruled out detached retinas and glaucoma but booked her for another kind of CT scan, because her left eye protruded and he wanted to check out whether anything was behind it. Meanwhile, Dr. Gray said, her blood pressure was way too high; this wasn't an easy time for her, he knew. What had she been doing in the evenings, how had she been coping? He had a way of looking at her as though he already knew, but he was a gent and let her confess in her own style. Because Christina liked her assignments in writing, he gave her a prescription slip on which he had printed in large block letters STOP ALL ALCO-HOL, and told her to report back in three weeks.

"And I wouldn't worry too much about the protruding eye. A lot of people have one eye that sticks out more than the other, but he's got to check it out. However, if you can't get your pressure down, we'll have to do something."

Back home, Christina took down the *New Yorker* cartoon that had enjoyed pride of place on their kitchen bulletin board long enough to have gone brown and curly at the edges. A couple sitting side by side on the sofa, drinks in hand. The man's free arm encircles the woman, who has kicked off her shoes and leans into his embrace. "I love these quiet evenings at home battling alcoholism," the woman is saying.

Christina tacked up Dr. Gray's block-lettered injunction in the vacant spot. She made herself a cranberry cider with crushed ice and seltzer and a carefully sliced circle of lime. Needing a ritual to signify her intention, she lugged the heavy blue gin bottle from its freezer home and poured its contents down the drain.

"Farewell, Your Majesty. It's time you completed your Scotland mourning and returned to your duties in London.

"*Arrivederci,* John Paul."

But she would not throw away the cartoon.

Now to get through the rest of the evening. She cleared out Rudy's medicines from the kitchen shelf to the left of the sink: the Lasix, the Toprol, the Procardia, the Zestril, the pain killers, the Nitrostat, chronicling in her memory what had led to what in the fifteen-year-long saga of Rudy's organs betraying one another and breaking down. The costly Procrit, still lying flat in the refrigerator, for when his kidneys, protesting the multiple myeloma, started to fail. She retraced the insidious transition, beginning in his sixties, when he went from being the one who dashed ahead up mountain trails and paused indulgently when she needed to stop and catch her breath until that sad afternoon when they were doing their back-and-forth walk across the flat causeway over the reservoir and he urged her to go on and finish alone: "I'll wait right here for your return." Off she went, while he sat on the causeway railing behind, keeping her in his sight. She walked quickly so she could reach the end faster and turn around and have him in her sight to walk back to again.

Dr. Gray had used the expression "blotto," which left less room to wriggle out of than the euphemisms she had grown up with. The lady who had spent the night under the piano at the country club in a pool of vomit had been tipsy. Dear Judge So-and-So, bless his heart, had been three sheets in the wind again.

The other word lately ascribed to her was

more flattering to ponder: Gilbert Mallow's calling her and Rudy "formidable."

Christina recalled the occasion last winter when the Mallows met Rudy. The local caterer, whom Rudy and Christina liked, was giving a small dinner party for his favorite customers. By then, Rudy was inking *nyet* all over his At-a-Glance diary, often as late as on the day of the appointment. Wasting time had become anathema to him. The prospect of being trapped in a boring gathering now triggered anxieties hitherto saved for being iced in on their hill or out of reach of 911. There was no bad weather forecast on the day of the party, but that morning Christina took the caterer's explicit directions and made a dry run to his house so Rudy would not be worrying all day that they might get lost after dark.

As always, they showed up punctually (*"Ponctualité est . . ."*), which meant they were the first to arrive. Rudy made his bows to the host, accepted a glass of champagne, and staked out a firm chair with an upright back. Christina sat

Rudy's desk and watch

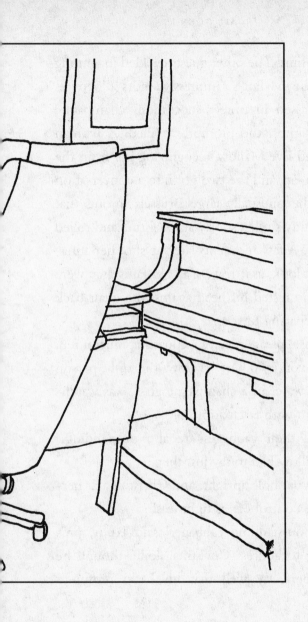

next to him. The other guests trickled in, among them the Mallows. Impressive hors d'oeuvres were passed in timely succession, champagne glasses almost too promptly refilled. A woman cornered Eve Mallow, recognizing her from the food co-op, and the two got into a conversation about the unusually large Brussels sprouts that year. Rudy smiled sourly at Christina and rolled his eyes. A few moments later he shot her a malevolent look, as if it were all her fault they were here, and rested his head against the chair back as if preparing to snooze.

"Please, please behave," Christina murmured, "I beg you." Gilbert Mallow, the only person sipping water in a champagne glass, was watching them with fascination.

"And their cabbages are also outstanding," Eve Mallow had to say just then.

Rudy sat bolt upright, and Christina felt herself lose control of his tight leash.

"An outstanding cabbage," said Rudy, pretending to address Christina alone, though he knew perfectly well that his basso profundo voice could silence a room, "would be a welcome addition to this gathering."

She had hated him fervently at that moment, so why was she now hooting with laughter until tears ran down her cheeks? The full force of his presence was often too much for her, especially when he was unleashing himself on his surroundings with that careless arrogance. But now the absence of that force she could never quite modify or control had left an excavation in her life that cried out to be filled with his most awful moments.

"It would be better to take a pill," Dr. Gray had said, "than to get blotto every evening. Better for your sleep patterns." He had given her a prescription for Ambien. "Start with half a pill and if that doesn't work, take the other half."

Christina abstained brilliantly for the three weeks until her next appointment. She had always responded well to a definite assignment. She took one or two of the Ambiens, then found herself falling asleep without them. When she went back to Dr. Gray, her blood pressure was normal and the CT scan results had come back negative and she had even lost four pounds.

But Dr. Gray looked sad and she told him so.

"I'm sad for you," he said. "I know some of what you must be feeling. My mother died ten years ago and I still miss her terribly. My father has never gotten over losing her. Tell me something: do you believe in an afterlife, that Rudy is up in heaven?"

"I did once, but I don't now," Christina admitted. "How about you?"

"I believe my mother's molecules are still part of the earth, and I know she lives on in me; she's with me every time I think of her," said Dr. Gray.

"I think of Rudy a lot," Christina said. "It sounds awful, but I pay more consistent attention to him now than I did when I had him right in front of me. I can hear exactly what he would say about so many things, the exact words and phrases and intonations. I must have absorbed a great deal of him in our years together."

Dr. Gray was watching her closely. "Look, Christina. Do you think you're going to make it through this?"

Christina considered a moment and replied honestly, "Yes, I think I am."

"We may never know what that blurred-vision episode was," Dr. Gray told her. "It could have been extreme hypertension. Or you may have passed a clot. Do you miss the alcohol?"

"Not desperately. I love the clarity, and I sleep better. But I'll probably have a glass of wine with friends over the holidays."

"Enjoy a glass with friends, but if I were you, I'd be very careful when you're at home alone" was Dr. Gray's parting advice.

Ralph the knife again

Chapter Six

Alcoholics Anonymous met at St. Aidan's on Tuesdays and Saturdays at five. Christina had often eavesdropped on them while weeding the church's perennial garden. If Rudy went along with her, he sat on a nearby bench, brooding fondly over her crouching form. Roars of applause erupted frequently from the open windows of the church hall. There was a certain exhibitionism about the proceedings, she and Rudy had agreed.

"The Pope will have left a message on the machine," Rudy would rumble complacently as they were driving home, about the same time that the AA group was having its coffee break, crushing out their cigarette butts in the newly weeded garden and hugging one another and tossing their Styrofoam cups and candy bar wrappers into the sand-filled clay urn the gardening committee had provided for their cigarette butts. Recently some abstainer had been taking out his rage on the folding metal chairs, bending them the wrong way till they broke, until Father Paul warned the group that if it didn't stop, they would have to meet elsewhere, as he was running out of chairs.

"I would rather die," Christina told Gilbert Mallow, who had stopped by to offer support at her newly abstemious cocktail hour while Eve was at the chiropractor's, "than stand up and give an accounting of myself to those people who stub their butts out in the church garden and abuse our poor chairs."

"There are more congenial groups," Gil told

her, sipping his herbal tea. "Or you may have the strength to go it alone. The one thing you cannot do, Christina, is make an exception—just that one little drinky-poo to get you through a party, the polite toast on someone's birthday. It's all over. Forever. Poison. You have to tell yourself that." In his eighteen years of sobriety, Gil had sampled many AA groups, from urbane Columbia professors to riverboat pilots (his favorite group), but now he walked. He walked in the country, but preferred the stimulation of populated streets. He and Eve kept a place in Manhattan, and sometimes he drove down to the city just to walk. "The rewards will be worth it, Christina. You'll find yourself getting words back. Whole rooms in your memory will open up." Gil had been, by his own admission, "a fall-down drunk," starting at age sixteen in prep school. Then when he was forty-nine he woke up one morning and couldn't tie his shoes. His first wife tied them for him and called a taxi, as he had also forgotten how to drive. When he got to his newspaper job, he couldn't connect the necessary mental circuits

for laying out the pages. His paper had good bene-
fits and he went off for six weeks to a renowned
drying-out establishment and hadn't touched a
drop since. Still, Christina resented being told *she*
could never have another drop.

Gil brought photographs of his late mother's
sculptures; he was preparing a major retrospective
at a Soho gallery. Christina was very interested in
Gertrude von Kohler Spezzi since she was going
to be buried next to her in the artists' cemetery.

"It's hard to get the feel of my mother's work
in these eight by tens," Gil said, lingering over
each photograph. He sat next to Christina on
the sofa, the hefty spiral portfolio resting on the
coffee table with his cup of herbal tea and her
cider and crushed ice with seltzer and lemon. At
sixty-seven, he had smooth, childlike hands with
almond-shaped nails gleaming with clear polish.
The Italian stepfather, his favorite of Gertrude's
husbands, had taught him the importance of
manicures. Gil with his high sloping forehead,
raisin-brown eyes, and neatly trimmed beard,
who wore buttoned-up dark shirts and light-

colored silk jackets, could have passed for a Mafia don himself, although his biological father had been an Anglican curate Gertrude had kept company with while studying stone reliefs in Romanesque churches in Sussex. "What is that funny-shaped vegetable on the altar?" Gertrude had asked Gil's father at his church's Harvest Festival. The curate, whose name Gertrude refused to share with her son, had replied, "It's a mallow," and so, back in Munich, when little swaddled Gil was presented to his mother in the lying-in hospital, Gertrude said he looked exactly like that funny mallow thing on the altar and put it down as his surname on the birth certificate. At this point, Gil's audience would express outrage or disbelief, and Gil would reward them with a sweet smile and say, "Wait, it gets worse."

Only, when Christina first heard the story, Rudy, seated directly across the long table from Gilbert Mallow at the caterer's dinner, had almost short-circuited things by rumbling, "Mallow? Isn't mallow a flower?"

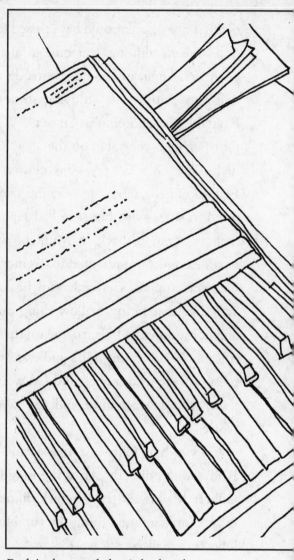

Rudy's phone and electric keyboard

"That's exactly what I meant when I said it gets worse," Gil had adroitly countered, rescuing his story by making it seem as though Rudy had supplied him with the perfect transition. "It wasn't until years later, after my Jungian analyst told me I should try to relate to my surname in a symbolic way since my mother refused to divulge the identity of my father. When I couldn't find a mallow in any of the vegetable books, I finally confronted my mother. She was in her eighties by then and mad as hell because she had shrunk four inches and her stone figures loomed over her. She laughed when I told her about my research and then she said, 'Come to think of it, Bertie, he might have said marrow, a vegetable *marrow,* that's what the English call an overgrown zucchini. Also, as I recall, the curate had trouble pronouncing his *r*'s. *Marrow* might well have come out of his mouth as "mawwow," and I thought I heard *mallow.* I wasn't completely bilingual in those days, you see.' "

"That Gilbert Mallow, or Marrow, was quite entertaining," Rudy pronounced as Christina drove them home from the caterer's dinner, which, due to the seating arrangements, had not been a disaster after all. Thanks to the Mallows, Rudy, himself like a rotund but breakable sculpture strapped upright into his seat for safe transport, was completely satisfied with the evening. "She's pretty, no fool, either, despite the outstanding cabbages. Of course, she's southern. You southerners consider it a point of honor to be able to discourse gracefully on everything from cockroaches to cabbages. Quite a legume-y evening, wasn't it? What a gorgon Gilbert's mother was. I've known women like that. There's only one way to treat them: laugh at them and walk away."

"Unless they're your mother," said Christina.

"True. But they supply prime-rib material for their children to dine out on."

While Gil was making her a second cranberry cider and seltzer, Christina leafed ahead in the thick portfolio of Gertrude von Kohler Spezzi's life-size sculptures of women, if you could call them that. At the worshipful pace Gil was taking, they would never make it through the portfolio. If the figures were this disquieting flattened on eight-by-ten glossy pages, what would it be like to stand in front of a three-dimensional one that was nearly six feet high? There was almost a fourth dimension of malevolence. You were always being warned by museum guards not to touch the Henry Moores, whose generous figures made you want to cuddle up beside them, but Gertrude's football-shouldered, sharp-hipped Valkyries with their high, wide-spaced afterthoughts of breasts had their own built-in alarm system: touch me and turn to stone yourself, or see an analyst for the rest of your life.

I am going to be lying next to that person, thought Christina. *Actually I will be lying just below her on the slope, as Rudy lies below her third husband, Simon Newman.* (Gertrude had kept her second husband's name, Spezzi.) *Rudy and I will lie side by side, his earthworms visiting mine. I can hear his voice coming through the side of my coffin as it used to reverberate through a closed door.*

"Well, my love, how's your old girl today?"

"*Too quiet,*" *I might call back.* "*I'm worried. What if Gertrude's starting to get depressed about all the love she missed out on while working so hard on her art? She's more fun when she's malevolent. How's your old guy?*"

"*Ah, poor Si. He refuses to get over how Whitmore junior beat him up and Mrs. Whitmore defended her son, saying he wouldn't touch a Jew with a ten-foot pole.*"

"*Well, but he's got his revenge,*" *I would reply.* "*Look who's in the Whitmore family's faces now.*"

Magnus Whitmore was the notoriously anti-Semitic founder of the village's arts colony in the twenties. Magnus's grave, at the foot of the grassy slope, was topped off by an imposing six-foot Della Robbia bas-relief of the Madonna and child, with a stone bench on either side of her. But since the burials of Si and Gertrude and Rudy, the whole setup now appeared as though the Madonna was guarding *their* graves, which were directly in the line of her protective gaze. And whoever sat on Magnus's benches would look up the rising slope and contemplate the stones of Si and Gertrude and Rudy, and one day Christina.

Gil came back with Christina's nondrink. "Oh, you've been looking ahead. I can tell you a story about that piece. When my mother was working on it—we'd emigrated to New York by then and I was home from my boarding school—in one of my pitiful bids for love I asked her why she hadn't just aborted me after her study trip in England. You know what she said? 'I didn't know there was anything wrong with me for six months.' She said she was always irregular from all her gymnastics as a girl, and when her body did begin to change shape after England she looked on it as an opportunity to experiment with more rounded forms in her work. She made dozens of plaster casts of her torso in the remaining months of pregnancy, but she said the results were too 'pudding-y' and she destroyed them. The subtext of that conversation was that in an artistic sense she *did* abort. But at least she credited me for saving her years of time. Because of me, she said, she found out early that roundness was to be avoided at all costs in her art. And then you know what she did? She took up her chisel and mallet and knelt down and started hollowing out the belly so that the pelvic bones would have those uncanny jutting edges so characteristic of her work."

Christina was imagining Gertrude von Kohler Spezzi's grimace of disgust as she applied cold wet plaster to her pregnant body. But wait a minute—who had knocked it off when it dried? However, she didn't think they had the time to go there, as Eve Mallow's chiropractor hour was almost up. And also, Christina was dying to be alone with Rudy, even though it was only the present-in-his-absence Rudy.

Rudy's downstairs study

Chapter Seven

*After Gil had gone, Christina decided to tackle some more letters of condolence, still coming in after seven months. She had them arranged in piles on Rudy's downstairs bed. When Rudy could no longer climb stairs, he'd moved to the room they'd built in case Christina's mother had to come and live with them when she was very old, but she had made a premature exit in a car accident. Yet they still called it "Mother's room," even after Rudy had been sleeping down there for five years.

In the priority pile were the notes and letters that had been most instructive to Christina, either because they opened up new possibilities for her connection with Rudy after death or because they provided models for future condolence letters she would be writing to others. Her first prize, so far, in the possibility category went to a woman who had written:

> A widowed friend of mine told me recently
> that, in his experience, love operates at a
> higher frequency after the death of the
> partner, and so it's easier to get through.

First prize, so far, in the model category (say something that connects the influence of the departed with the future of the world) went to the wife of Dr. Gray:

> I remember several years ago at a concert I
> told Rudy about our daughter's early attempts

with the flute. He encouraged me to start
her immediately with private lessons so she
wouldn't develop bad habits. Beth is now
on her way to becoming an accomplished
musician. Had it not been for Rudy's
prompting, I might not have acted so quickly.

Christina picked out a deserving note from
another fiction writer, a woman who had been
at Yaddo the summer Christina and Rudy met
and set fire to their respective lives in order to be
together.

The card, from the Metropolitan Museum of
Art, was a reproduction of a page of Chinese
characters from a T'ang dynasty album. It was
called "Spiritual Flight Sutra."

Dear Christina,

This is a very late note to say how sorry I
was to hear of Rudy's death. I remember the
two of you at Yaddo in the summer of 1972,
seeing you walk around the lake with your arms
linked. You two were the romance of the

summer. Such a loss must be hard to bear and
you have my sympathy. I hope and pray you
will soon be able to write again.

Christina took out a note card with her name
engraved on it and covered the front and back of
it in her slanty convent script, saying more than
she had planned and having to write in the space
up the sides.

Dear Lauren,
    Thank you for your kind note. He was a big
man and he leaves a big space. I miss having
Bach played while I prepare dinner. You will be
glad to hear I never stopped writing. It was
what I did for twenty-eight years while he was
making up music under the same roof and it is
good to go up every morning and keep doing
it, just as if he were still downstairs. I miss
hearing his little bursts of melody and all the
rest that goes with capturing it, but in a way I
still do hear. Recently, I went looking for his
metronome and was surprised to discover that it

Rudy's chair again

wasn't the wooden pyramid kind I'd thought, but a little quartz thing the size of a remote control garage opener. Now it lives on my desk next to my ragged old thesaurus and before I boot up my computer every morning I turn it on. It's still set at the tempo he left it on, his last workday in this house: 94, smack dab in the middle of andante. *Pock-pock-pock-pock*, like a lively heartbeat, with the little red light flashing. It's very comforting, and I sometimes feel I am purloining some of the pulsing energy of his music and his strong personality.

Perhaps she could handle one more deserving note. Oops, this one was six months old, from the student of Rudy's who gave him the brass elephant.

I was in the practice room one afternoon improvising a tune when my professor stuck his head in and said, "Young man, you'd do better to go up to the library and listen to some Beethoven." I went on improvising,

though my spirits were dampened, and after
a while Professor Geber stuck his head in the
door and said in that unforgettable voice:
"Try it in B-flat, it might work better." It
did, and I transferred to his class. I am the
one who gave him the brass elephant when
he retired. He wrote me a letter I will always
cherish, saying he kept it on his desk at
home and every time he touched it he
thought of me.

That one will have to wait a little longer, Christina
thought, choking up. *I can't rise to it tonight.* Lauren's note had brought back their whole opening scene, like having time's tail whip you in the
face.

Christina's study phone

Chapter Eight

That cold and rainy afternoon in June of 1972, cocktail time in the fifty-five-room mansion at Saratoga Springs. The artists in residence, in jeans or other studiedly funky getups, are gathered in the downstairs library, a fussy Victorian room with velvet furniture and novels by late-nineteenth-century popular authors and volumes of poetry by Henry Van Dyke. There's a lady celebrating her eighty-first birthday, a novelist who writes generational novels about

Jewish families in Brooklyn, and she's wearing a blue-and-white patterned dress and nice jewelry and has stocked the bar with bottles of Scotch, bourbon, gin, rum, and white wine, along with the appropriate mixers, so all can have their choice of libations. There are also little dishes of nuts and pretzels, set out by the octogenarian novelist, whose name is Zelda.

Christina, wearing brown strap sandals with stacked heels, bell-bottomed khaki jeans with a button fly, her grandmother's gold-and-seed-pearl pendant, shaped like a tiny grape cluster, hanging demurely on its fragile chain just below the V of her faded salmon-colored T-shirt, has arranged herself, mermaid style, on a velvet chaise longue the color of saffron, and sips a Scotch and water, trying to look like a reserved novelist shrewdly summing people up. She celebrated her thirty-fifth birthday (prime rib and two beers) three evenings before at a Ramada Inn in Erie, Pennsylvania, en route to this artists' retreat, where she has been invited to stay for two full months. On the door of her motel

room was a decal of a smiling masked thief tip-
toeing away with a bag over his shoulder: PLEASE
DO NOT LEAVE VALUABLES IN CAR.

Although she was exhausted from her all-day
drive from Iowa City, where she was on tenure
track at the university, she dragged herself out to
her blue 1970 Mustang, the car she would still
be dreaming about as her ur-car thirty years
later, and unloaded the rest of her valuables: her
blue IBM Selectric (which she would belt into
the Mustang's bucket seat on the passenger side
and drive off with in high dudgeon every time
she and Rudy had a big fight for the next ten
years, until both machines were replaced and the
fights got less dramatic); two months' worth of
ribbons and correction tapes; her cheap typing
paper and her two reams of twenty-pound
bond; her *Webster's New World Dictionary, College
Edition*; her brand-new hardbound *Roget's International Thesaurus, Third Edition* ("You look so
happy with your purchase!" a professor's wife
had called to Christina as she came out of Iowa
Book and Supply, and Christina will often think

of that woman in years to come when she's opening her taped-up, threadbare old standby to find a better word, or track down one she's forgotten).

Christina clinks the two ice cubes in her Scotch and water and sums up her fellow artists. Some are sweet but not very interesting; most, including herself, are still hungry strivers, a few, including a sneering nasal-voiced twelve-tone composer who told her melody was the enemy, are downright obnoxious. Only old Zelda seems secure in her bounty.

Since arriving at the mansion, Christina has written fifteen new pages on her novel about three generations of women. She is on page 149 of the book, part one, the grandmother's story. Part one takes place in 1905, only twelve years after this mansion was built. The scheming housekeeper who will marry the father and steal the two sisters' legacy has just walked in the door of the farmhouse, wearing her black bombazine dress and carrying her carpetbag. Christina will make herself finish this section, getting through the night the grandmother's sister runs away with the villain in a traveling melodrama passing through the southern mountain town. Then on to part two, the mother's story, though the author is dying to get to part three.

Years later, part one will exist only in typescript in the university archive where Christina has deposited her papers. Part two will never get written. While still at the mansion—Christina and Rudy having burned their bridges and made public their intentions (too public, according to the twelve-tone composer, who was reported to have added, "But the Chosen People work fast")—Christina will abandon the grandmother's and the mother's generations and start the book all over again in present time, writing in a different way: filling in and rounding out as she goes, attending to the sensibilities of the moment rather than trudging chronologically from preplanned point to point. While still at the mansion, Rudy will pack in his tongue-in-cheek attempts to outsmart the Boulez crowd and instead begin a major choral work of sweeping emotional grandeur based on William Blake's

The villa, the orphanage, the factory

"Four Zoas," to which Christina has introduced him. Before she has to leave the mansion to resume her teaching duties in Iowa, Rudy will have sketches of the first two songs to play for her: "It is an easy thing to triumph in the summer sun," and "O, Prince of Death, where art thou?" She will leave her volume (*The Poetry and Prose of William Blake*) behind with him in Saratoga Springs, and it is to reside on his shelves in the three houses they live in for the next twenty-eight years.

Toward the end of the cocktail hour, there is a sudden flurry in the library, a galvanizing of the room's molecules as a tall red-haired man blazes in like a brushfire.

"So, Zelda, what's new?" he demands in a voice lower than God's, and the old lady murmurs something confidentially in his ear as she turns away from the room to mix his drink. Just neat Scotch, he tells her, it's been an awful two days, he's been in Manhattan doing a recording session with a bunch of tone-deaf fools. ("There's a new writer here from Iowa" is what Zelda has murmured. "She's nice, though she poses a little.")

"That's the composer Rudolf Geber," says a novelist named Lauren, who has joined Christina on the velvet chaise longue. The twelve-tone composer, standing above the women, says in his snide nasal voice: "He's very arrogant."

Christina looks over to see if the arrogant composer in his yellow polo shirt with the glasses jammed in the pocket has overheard the remark. He's standing next to Zelda, looking straight at Christina from under his lowering shaggy eyebrows. ("I find you the most fascinating person I have ever met," he will tell her ten days hence, slapping at his and her mosquitoes with his free hand as they walk arm in arm around the lake, "and I've got a good notion to throw everything else out the window, except my work of course. It would be the intelligent thing to do, and I'm the sort to do it.")

At dinner, he sits down beside her and begins plying her with questions. His mind ranges all over the place like a searchlight, seeking out the corners where she usually has to play by herself. If arrogance is the refusal to squander yourself on the unpassionate and the unfascinating, then he is arrogant. But toward her there is a generosity of spirit she recognizes as rare, an attention that is larger than self-consciousness. The world around them is soon canceled, but nevertheless, after dinner, when he asks Christina to join him for a walk on the terrace, she feels something close to terror and says she has to go upstairs and work some more.

As she climbs the baronial staircase to her room, she can't resist looking back at him. He has opened the French doors and gone outside by himself. Back and forth he marches on the blustery terrace, as if he owns the place, red hair rippling in the wind, yellow shirt blazing through the gloaming, canvasing the lay of the land from under his shaggy brows.

It's as though he's known exactly the moment she will look back. With a sweeping motion of his arm, he is summoning her to change her mind and join him. She can see his mouth shaping the words: "Come out."

She manages a nervous wave and keeps climbing the stairs. Safe in her room, she brushes her teeth with a tingly spearmint toothpaste and settles down in her bed to read some more of *Daniel Deronda*. Eventually she turns out the light and falls asleep. She dreams that she is walking along a street with her present lover, the one who awaits her back in Iowa City. Suddenly she looks up and there is the arrogant red-haired composer, standing in an open upstairs window filled with green plants. He is motioning to her: "Come up."

"Sorry," she says to the lover. "I have to go."

Facing south at kitchen sink in morning

Chapter Nine

Christina wandered into Rudy's study and turned on his desk lamp. She trailed her fingers along his closed Yamaha grand (he had bought it the day after he watched Laurence Olivier's deathbed scene in *Brideshead Revisited*: "What am I waiting for? If not now, when?").

She sat down at his desk and stroked the cool flanks of the brass elephant, perusing the day's junk mail she had placed on Rudy's desk earlier, an indulgence she continued to allow herself (along with his recorded telephone message, which she could not bring herself to erase).

Today's mail that had not needed to be forwarded to Rudy's executor had included a letter from Verizon, with its priceless boast in red on the envelope: WE HAVE PULLED OUT ALL THE STOPS TO GET YOU TO COME BACK!

Christina gave an appreciative snort and slid the envelope beneath Rudy's Seiko watch, still on Daylight Saving Time from last April, and admired her arrangement. The composition of the two objects gave her a visceral satisfaction, perhaps akin to that experienced by her grave-neighbor-to-be, Gertrude von Kohler Spezzi, when she had scooped out another inch of belly from a stone torso.

Bud announced his return from the great beyond. He shot through the door when she opened it, and protested angrily when she didn't follow him to the kitchen but instead flung herself out into the freezing December evening.

"Ah, Christ, Rudy, enough is enough!" Christina yelled. "Verizon wants you back and so do I!"

A lonely dog answered from somewhere below. She returned to the house and lit some candles, humming a swatch of an unidentifiable hymn. She caught herself humming almost constantly now, as if to compensate for the abrupt withdrawal of music from her life.

She picked up the cat's dish, scraped off the dried food, rinsed it and placed it in the dishwasher, got a clean dish, opened a can of Salmon in Chunks for Feline Seniors, making a little pas de deux with Bud as he wound himself in and out of her legs.

Only after he had flattened his elegant tail and hunkered down to take nourishment did she genuflect on one knee and gaze beseechingly into the crannies of the wine rack.

A last bottle of Gigondas, placed there months ago by Rudy's living hand, suddenly materialized and nuzzled its neck into the welcoming curl of her fingers. ("Enjoy a glass of wine with friends," Dr. Gray had said, "but I'd be careful when you're home alone.")

No, it's not easy, my love, when you've outgrown or

*outlived all your authority figures. But you're strong. I
remember the time I picked up your hand in the coffee
bar in Saratoga Springs. They were playing that popular tune stolen from the Mozart G-minor. We had just
decided to set fire to the status quo and be together for
the rest of our lives. "Your hand is astonishingly soft,"
I told you, "but the grip is like steel." You'll work it
out, if I know you—you'll make your own rules. The
Cope palled and now you'll invent your own rituals.*

"Ah, Rudy, Rudy, Rudy."

Assuming he was the one being addressed,
Bud answered with an upbeat Siamese syllable.

"You couldn't walk around the house anymore
without stopping for breath, but you could still pop
the cork on champagne and open a bottle of wine."

Bud vouchsafed another syllable and then
segued into his "going out" command.

*("Don't look at me like that. I want a decision on
your part. Just make up your mind and I'll do whatever you ask. You want to sit there. All right."*

Christina had been in her study one summer
morning when Rudy's voice, an octave below
God's, came floating up to her. He was standing

. . . the pasha's daughter's glass

at the front door, reasoning with Bud, who was deciding whether or not he wished to go out. She had snatched up a pencil and scribbled the words on the yellow pad beside her computer because of their quintessential Rudy-ness—she knew they would give her a pleasure and a pang to reread someday.)

Christina accompanied Bud back to the door and he swished out expectantly into the star-filled winter night.

Back in the kitchen, she reached into an uppermost corner of the cupboard and eased forward Rudy's cordial glass with the etched grapes, given to him by the pasha's daughter in Cairo. She drew forth its elegant shape, held it up to the light, then wiped it lovingly with a fresh dish towel, the way Father Paul wiped the chalice with the purificator after communion.

Across the street from Christina's childhood home had lived a reclusive old lady, all by herself, in a big ocher stuccoed house, half hidden by overgrown shrubs. Mrs. Carruthers. Mr. Carruthers had been dead longer than most people's memories. Sometime after five each evening, Mrs. Carruthers's middle-aged son, Freddie, who worked at the bank, would park his black Packard in his mother's driveway and dart behind the shrubbery carrying a brown paper bag twisted at the top. A half hour or so later he would emerge, carrying the same bag, twisted at the top, and drive away. Everyone knew what was in the bag and everyone knew the pact Mrs. Carruthers had made with her solitary life. The bag contained a bottle of wine. Inside the house, Freddie uncorked the bottle, measured exactly half of its contents into his father's old cut-glass decanter, poured his mother her first glass, and drove off with the recorked bottle to his own house, which he shared with another bachelor who worked in the library. The next evening, Freddie would arrive punctually and pour the rest of the previous day's bottle into the decanter. On the third evening he would bring a new bottle and start the process over again.

"Well, the sun has just set over the yardarm," Christina's mother would announce when Freddie's Packard pulled in across the street.

"Do you think they buy it for her by the case or what?" Christina's grandmother wondered.

"They certainly can't buy anything decent around here," Christina's mother would say. "They probably stock up when they go on their little trips to Atlanta."

Rudy had loved this story and often told it to people. He was fascinated by southern speech and manners and the secrets they covered up yet didn't cover up.

Christina measured exactly one full portion into Rudy's cordial glass. Then she recorked the Gigondas (which Rudy had chosen because it was called "Oratorio") and scrutinized its remaining level. Four evenings' worth, if she was careful. (This advice is included in the price of the story.)

"And then I'll go from there, creating my

own rituals. Taking possession, in nightly incre-
ments, of all you meant to me."

For the second time since Rudy's death,
Christina sat down in his magisterial Stickley
armchair on the other side of the fireplace.

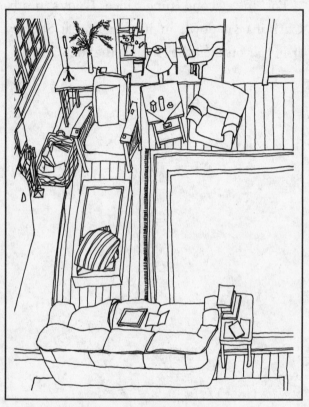

Christina's sofa, Rudy's chair

Chapter Ten

The first time in the chair had been back in April, just after Christina had finished with her seven days of shiva-salons and was alone again in the evenings.

Father Paul and Eliza, a parishioner she especially liked, had showed up around five to see how she was getting on, and after a few minutes of warm, intelligent, dry-eyed conversation with them, Christina found herself whooping and wailing and totally out of control.

"I just wish I knew where he was," she managed to blurt between sobs.

"Have you prayed?" asked Father Paul.

"I'm not sure I can."

"Have you asked Rudy to help you?"

"No."

"Have you read the Burial Office?"

"No."

"Would you like to do that now?"

"Yes."

While Father Paul went out to his car to get his Bible and *The Book of Common Prayer,* Eliza snuggled up next to Christina on the sofa and wept with her like a sister in grief. A year ago Eliza had had to leave her dying father's bedside in England in order to fly home to her husband, who had just had a stroke.

"If only I had known it was our last night together," Christina choked out, "I would have stayed with him."

"I know, I know," said Eliza. "You wanted to be there. All this time you've been with him and you feel you let him down at the end. You feel like the disciples did about falling asleep in the garden."

"Where should I sit?" Christina asked Father Paul when he returned.

"Where would you like to sit?" he asked.

And that was when she chose Rudy's chair.

Father Paul dropped cross-legged to the floor like a yogi and spread his open books out on the altar of the coffee table. Eliza sat in the black leather chair, which, for some reason, unlike its matching sofa, had escaped the ravages of the cats.

"We'll take this slowly," said Father Paul, and waited while Christina went through another cycle of wild crying and gasping. While her body was succumbing to these paroxysms, her mind coolly registered how impatient she had been all her life and how she projected this impatience onto others: *Surely Eliza must be dying to get home to Jack, and Father Paul has had a long day and wishes I would pull myself together so we could get on with it and he could go home and have his supper.*

But Father Paul gave no signs of wanting to get

on with it. When he did begin reading the burial service and selections from scripture, it was in an alert, rather surprised way, as though he were coming upon the words himself for the first time.

It was new for Christina not to follow along in the prayer book, rushing ahead with her eyes. She allowed the words to pass over or soak into her as they saw fit.

Bud crouched solemnly on the rug, very much a part of the gathering. At one point, he arose, stretched sinuously, and ambled off to the kitchen, from where they could hear him slowly crunching his dry food. Presently, he returned and took up his former pose, a neatly folded cat.

"Hope that is seen is not hope," Father Paul read from Romans. "Why hope for what is already seen? But if we hope for what we do not see, we wait for it with eagerness and patience."

Now, on this December night early in the eighth month after Rudy's death, Christina, in his chair, raised his/her glass (what is the sound of one glass toasting?) and took a determined but rational sip of the Gigondas "Oratorio."

"To hope," she said, gazing at her own absent place on the sofa. "What did you see when I was sitting over there, two yards away from you?"

"I saw you, my love. In your varied manifestations. In your married vanifestations."

"I've missed you. There were things left unfinished. I thought we would have the summer together. You said, 'We still have some more time together.' Your last words to me. Did you really think so?"

"I hoped so."

"I went home and read a novel. I was never able to finish it afterward. It's not her fault, but I won't ever read that writer again. I read until two or three in the morning. You were sinking but I didn't know it. I'm glad you had Edward, the same nurse who was with you eleven Aprils ago when, as you put it, 'I made my maiden voyage to intensive care.'

"Edward said I could call him at home and he told me all I wanted to hear, which was everything. How delighted you were to see him when he came on duty. How you filled him in on the intervening years, our trip to Sweden for my book, the last time we traveled together, what you had been writing, the operas and musical plays we wrote together.

" 'But then,' you told him, 'my life slowly changed and I could do less and less.'

"Around ten, you had chest pains. The heart doctor ordered a drip of nitro and some morphine. You settled down and slept some. Toward morning, your oxygen started dropping, more diuretics were administered, a blood test showed dialysis was needed. Your kidney doctor was on vacation, so his associate came and you signed the papers. Then your blood pressure began to drop, your breathing got shallow, they administered more diuretics, and when the doctor was putting in the catheter for dialysis, your heart rate dropped and you lost consciousness: not enough oxygen to the brain, Edward explained. They called code blue, the crash cart came, all your numbers were sky high, the pH of your blood changed, and Edward and the other nurses realized at a certain point in the resuscitation that they had just lost you.

" 'We were devastated,' he said. 'We stood around the bed holding hands. We were in a daze. This man was affecting all of us. His energy was still there.'

" 'He's a man I'll never forget,' said Edward. 'I was surprised that a man so sick could maintain such a high level of consciousness right to the end.'

"You were conscious enough to bring your life story to completion, with Edward as the listener.

"At seven-thirty the phone woke me. I picked it up, expecting your rumbly voice, instructing me what to bring, sweater, socks, in case they were keeping you another day.

"But a stranger asked for me by name, and when I said, 'Speaking,' he identified himself as the doctor on duty at the ICU. 'I have bad news,' he said. 'Rudy didn't make it.'

" 'Do you mean he's dead?' For those few seconds I guess I was still clinging to the thinnest semantic thread: 'didn't make it' maybe meaning you'd lost consciousness or not responded, something just short of hopeless, but on this side of death.

"But no.

"Then I heard myself asking, 'Is it all right if I come and see him anyway?'

"When I got to the ICU, a nurse came out, weeping, and asked me to wait a few more minutes outside your room—four-fifteen—while she finished 'getting you ready.' I stood with my back to the nurses' station, facing your partially closed door, hugging my purse to my chest and reciting Hail Marys to regulate my breathing. I could catch glimpses of her moving efficiently back and forth from bed to sink to waste container, cleaning up after the crash cart exertions. Then she said I could come in.

"Your skin was still warm. Your cheeks and chin were stubbled with fresh growth and there was a bandage around your neck with a trace of dried blood. Your body in the blue-and-white patterned hospital gown was more rotund than before, obviously swollen, as was your face, which gave it the fullness of complacency.

"You weren't there, anybody could see that. But you had left behind an expression of . . . how to describe it? Superiority? Bemusement beyond caring? A distanced, tranquil amusement? Satisfaction at a task completed?

"The nurse went out, and I touched your face and then your hands, which could bring forth such complicated sounds, and which, for the first time, did not respond to my touch with a squeeze or a grasp. I looked away, then back, half expecting I could surprise you into a change of expression.

"It was my first experience of looking at you when I couldn't influence how you looked back at me.

"Now I have to make the crossover between image and presence. The funny thing is, I can still *hear* the essential you, though I miss having you in my sight. I, the visual one, now have to rely on sounds."

Coda

─────────

I used to try to be original," you said about your
work, not long before you died. "Now I try to
be clear and essential."

About Bach, you remarked, at the end of a day
when you'd had another transfusion, "He has order
and stability, qualities one doesn't always have in one's
life. Yet he's not predictable, sentimental, or personal."

And then there was the night, in our last months
together, when I sat over there on the sofa and regaled

you at length about all my fears: about my work, about the future, about my fear of losing you.

Later, after I was upstairs in bed, and you were in one of your commutes between the refrigerator and a late movie in your study, you called up to me:

"Hello? Are you still awake?"

"Yes," I called back. "Why?"

"Bud is sitting right outside your door. He's protecting you from all evil and danger."

Possible Sins

At the age of eleven, Christina, along with seven other girls and boys, knelt in her turn before the bishop, who flattened her crown of curls with his weighty consecrated hand and admitted her into the Anglican Communion. Having entered what the Prayer Book called her Years of Discretion, she would be able to march up to the rail with the grown-ups and swallow a convent-produced wafer of unleavened bread followed by a sip of New York State

port and return to her seat with downcast eyes
and folded hands. She also was now eligible to
partake of the even more mysterious sacrament
of confession. With the Eucharist, you could
watch others and create your own style from
their bad and good examples: *not* like the
scrunched piousness of Mrs. Dottie Cameron,
whose clenched hands seemed to be shielding
her lower female parts, but more like tall, handsome Ida Griffin, with her dashing silver
cowlick, who carried her hands waist high and
proudly lifted out from her body like the singer
she was.

But confession was in secret, just Father Weir
and you in the brown confessional box at the
back of the church, and, curious as she was,
Christina would not get caught eavesdropping
to learn how others went about it. Imagination
would have to serve here: Dottie Cameron in a
hunch of contrition, secretly pleased with her
grocery list of sins, whispering urgently at Father's ear on the other side of the screen; handsome Ida (whose short marriage had been

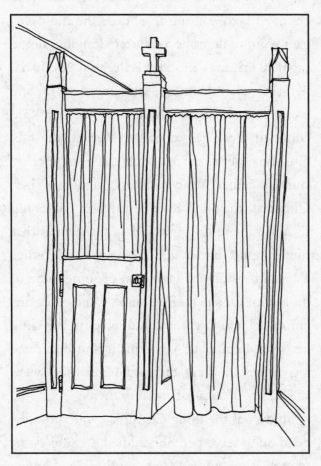

Confessional

dissolved) folded on her long legs into the cramped box, pausing to choose the most elegant word to describe a spinster's longings in the night. Christina's mother, Kate, told lies, social lies, she called them, the kind necessary for any woman alone in the world, but whether Kate admitted these lies to Father Weir in the box Christina very much doubted. Her mother wanted Father Weir to think highly of her. Christina imagined Kate in the box confessing to more interesting spiritual sins, the ones that might result in an appointment with Father Weir in his study and the loan of some more of his books. Or she might confess some other sins entirely. Though she and Kate slept in the same bed every night, and Christina had made a catalog of her mother's different sighs, there were still plenty of areas of mystery there.

Study was the thing Christina could most depend on to serve her. She studied her subjects in school, she studied her mother, and now, preparing for her first confession, she studied the pamphlet put out by the Order of the Holy

Cross, "How to Make Your Confession." The Self-Examination for Children, a mere page, was like being handed a child's menu in a restaurant when your appetite had swollen beyond those junior portions. ("Been rude, sulky, or cross? Told or listened to impure stories? Laughed at others for doing right?")

She plunged with enthusiasm into the heartier fare of adult sins, but soon grew disappointed, then dejected.

"I confess to Almighty God, to all the saints, and to you, Father. . . ."

The hour had come. She was in the box and could smell his Old Spice aftershave on the other side of the screen. Her hand jiggled a little as she squinted at her checkmarked pamphlet in the gloom. "I'll do the children's part first, even though I'm no longer a child. I've done everything on the children's page, except cheated in school. But I don't need to cheat so I'm not sure that counts. Well, here goes with the adult part. Under Pride, I've been self-conscious, conceited, annoyed when corrected,

Interior of confessional

called attention to myself, exaggerated, gossiped, and ridiculed others. Under Envy, I've delighted in the failures of others and grieved at the attainment of others. Under Covetousness, well, again, most of the sins have to do with using money wrongfully, so I don't know yet. I mean, I haven't got any. Anger, I've checked all of those except 'been guilty of any violent action.' No, I once threw smelling salts at my mother's face because she was reading and wouldn't answer me. Under Lust, I'm not sure if this counts as an impure thought but lately I've been, well, *concentrated* on people's sexual life. I mean I just look at someone and wonder about what they do, or don't do in that department. But I hope to outgrow this soon."

All too soon she reached the end of all the categories on the adult list. "For these and all other sins," she read from the pamphlet, "which I cannot now remember, I am truly sorry. . . ." And now she was asking for absolution. She felt thoroughly let down.

"Is there anything else?" Father Weir asked.

"I guess not, but it seems there should be more."

"Would you care to enlarge on that?"

"Oh, I don't know. If I were God, I would want to really show someone how much I could forgive. This is just peanuts. Murder isn't even on here. It's all such piddling *neighborhood* stuff. It's stupid. I think God must be bored out of his mind, if this is all adults have to confess. I thought there would be more possibilities."

"For his mercy to sink its teeth into, you mean?"

"Well, yes! Exactly."

Then Father Weir, before he pronounced absolution, said something to Christina that made her feel powerful and chosen for the remainder of her youth and beyond.

Years later, when he was an old man and she was far along in adulthood, they were having lunch in a restaurant and Father Weir was saying he was ready to be translated into the next world anytime. This led to a playful-but-

Father Weir's and Christina's lunch

serious dialogue about whether the dead could send messages back to the living, and if such a message arrived how could you make sure it was authentic. He said it might go through a third party's dream, perhaps, but there would have to be a password known only to the dead person and the recipient of the message.

"How about what you said to me that time in the confessional," said Christina.

"Refresh my memory."

"That I had it in me to be a great saint or a great sinner. That has given me strength for years."

"I recollect saying something of the sort," he said with a smile.

"We could use that as our password," Christina said.

"It's a bit long," said Father Weir. He pointed at his plate. "Why not just—"

He pronounced the name of the favorite thing he always ordered when they came to this restaurant and they agreed on that.

Largesse

hristina had a rich aunt she had never met, her mother's first cousin, actually. Aunt Demaris lived on a ranch in Alabama part of the year and on a ranch in Texas the other part. She and her cattleman husband had not been blessed, as she put it, with children. Her Christmas presents to Christina, which usually arrived before Thanksgiving, were lavish and sometimes completely inappropriate. Christina was allowed to open them at once because her mother and grandmother were just as curious as she was to see what was inside.

One Christmas a sizable box arrived from Maison Blanche in New Orleans. Excavating through postal paper, store gift wrapping, and tissue paper, all of which the grandmother folded and saved, they confronted what at first appeared to be some flattened exotic animal. But no, it was a child's coat of spotted fur with matching hat and muff.

"She's out of her mind," said Christina's mother, "this is *leopard* skin. And it's her handwriting on the card, so it's not some hired shopper's folly this time."

"The child can't possibly wear this to school," said the grandmother. "And she certainly can't wear it to church."

"Perhaps they haven't heard at Maison Blanche or out at the ranches that there's a war on," remarked Christina's mother in the low deadpan voice she employed for her caustic mode.

They gave the coat, hat, and muff to the cleaning woman's little daughter. Christina's grandmother lied tactfully that the coat was too tight
in the arms for Christina, and that of course the
hat and muff must stay part of the ensemble.
Christina never tried on the coat, nor did she remember wanting to. The thank-you note had to
be written all the same, and she went to work on
it on Christmas Day, after the presents had all been
opened and there was a sad lull in the living room.
Her grandmother was doing a crossword puzzle.
The Christmas Day edition of the local newspaper rested on her mother's lap; she had been
rereading the interviews she had done with the
wounded servicemen at the local military hospital.

"So far I've got *Dear Aunt Demaris,*" Christina
said glumly.

"That's an opener," said Christina's mother.
"Be thankful I didn't name you Demaris."

"You wouldn't have!"

"She hinted. But I said your father had his
heart set on Christina."

"He did?" Christina's father had been out of the picture since her infancy and she was always interested in more information about him when her mother was willing to volunteer it.

"No. He wanted to name you Greta."

"Why?"

"Oh, after Garbo. I don't know."

"Dear Aunt Demaris. Thank you so much for the—WHAT? Help me!"

"You need an adjective," said her mother.

"I think I used *wonderful* last year."

"Let's see: *remarkable, unusual, unprecedented . . .*" Her mother uttered a snort and lost control. "Thank you so much for that unprecedented disaster of a coat." They both dissolved into wild laughter.

When they had finished, the grandmother, without looking up from her puzzle, suggested, "How about *grand*? Thank you so much for the grand coat."

"Mother, that's just inspired!" Christina's mother exclaimed in sincere admiration.

"I must get something out of my crosswords," replied the grandmother.

Liberalities from the unmet aunt in Texas marked successive Christmases: the filigree and pearl music box that played "Toora Loora Loora"; the gold mesh bracelet studded with heart-shaped diamond chips that Christina admired on her wrist until she lost it in midsummer; the brocaded kimono-bathrobe with its big sleeves that caught on doorknobs; the rabbit fur jacket, worn once to a dance and then packed away. Christina's thank-you notes got easier, as did her command of adjectives most likely to impress and please. After Aunt Demaris requested it, she always enclosed a school picture of herself.

When Christina was fifteen, Aunt Demaris wrote, or rather her secretary wrote and Aunt Demaris signed the letter in her ornamented script, inviting Christina to spend Christmas with them at their Texas ranch. While the mother and

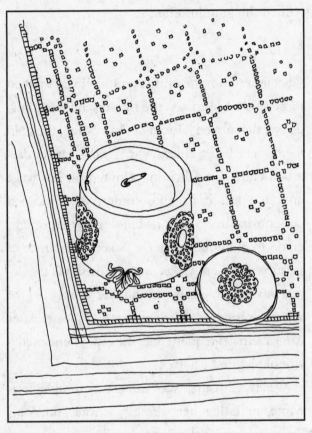

The filigree and pearl music box that played
"Toora Loora Loora"

grandmother were debating over what to do, a telegram arrived: ALL EXPENSES PAID OF COURSE STOP PHONE COLLECT STOP EAGER TO HEAR.

"Well, here it comes," said the grandmother.

"Pandora's box," Christina's mother enigmatically murmured. "What about it, Christina? It's your invitation. Would you like to go?"

"I don't know, I guess it would be an experience." Christina tried to picture how the older couple would go about entertaining her. She was pretty sure there would be shopping. She hoped her uncle would not expect her to ride a horse well.

The phone call was made, not collect, the mother and grandmother were too proud, but then they regretted it. First a maid who couldn't speak English answered and had to go and get another maid who could, and then Aunt Demaris was "detained" for a while longer. When at last her cousin came on the phone, Christina's mother's face crunched between the eyebrows and, looking strained, she started speaking in a funny way. At first it sounded like a parody of someone being gushy, but later she explained to Christina that Aunt Demaris brought that out in you. After Christina's mother finished the phone call, she declared herself exhausted and went to lie down.

The airplane ticket arrived, followed by a huge package from Neiman Marcus. Inside was a white Samsonite suitcase and inside the suitcase were a black velvet skirt and top, a turquoise velvet cummerbund, a black taffeta slip, and dangling earrings of turquoise and hammered gold.

"I suppose she trusts us enough to supply the proper underclothes," the grandmother remarked as she carefully folded the tissue paper.

In the weeks preceding the trip, they crammed Christina with Demaris stories, some she heard before, but this time with an extra deliberateness, as though they were preparing her for some kind of test.

"She was always strong-willed," said the grandmother. "Even before her parents were killed. She was my husband's little niece. He and his brothers helped raise her in their mother's boardinghouse. This was when they were all struggling to make ends meet. The boys worked in the iron mines and came home every morning with rust-colored skin, and the mother cooked for the boarders and changed their sheets. But they treated Demaris like a princess, and I guess she just assumed that's what she was. When she was sixteen she made them all become Roman Catholics. All but my husband, he was in the Masons, you know, and had to refuse her. Then she met Karl, he was from a family of German immigrants, just a young assistant in a butcher shop. She made *him* become a Catholic and taught him math and good English and next thing you know they owned a meat market, and they branched out into cattle and before they knew it they were millionaires. Demaris credited their good fortune completely to the Lord, but she was always very appreciative of my husband's family. Though she never warmed to me. I was too reserved, I guess, the way mountain people are. And I wouldn't play cards with them on Sunday when we visited down in Alabama."

"I think the math and good English ought to get some credit for the fortune, too," said Christina's mother. "Though, good English? I'm not so sure. Look at me and all *my* English— where has it gotten me?"

Christina's mother drove her a hundred and fifty miles across the state so that she could fly to Texas without having to change airplanes. This was possible because the junior college where she taught English for not enough money was on Christmas break. Despite her brilliant feature stories (what other local reporter could have interviewed Béla Bartók in French?) she had been let go from the newspaper after the war so that the men could have their jobs back. In her low moods, she could be quite caustic about this.

Christina's mother had turned down the grandmother's offer to come along. This made it into an adventure, since the two had never traveled anywhere alone. Mother and daughter left before dawn, while the stars were winking in the black winter sky. Aromas from the bacon and egg sandwiches and the Thermos of coffee, packed by the grandmother, wafted enticingly from the backseat of the old car, bought new in a more prosperous era, when the grandmother's husband was alive. As they wound down the steep curves of the mountain roads and the sky began to lighten beyond the ranges, Christina's mother suddenly began to talk with a strange urgency about the father who had been out of the picture since her infancy. "He was just so damned handsome and charming and equally unsuitable, but I wanted him, and I got him. By the time you were on the way, I knew it wasn't going to work. But I still wanted you. Daddy was still alive and he and mother wanted you, too."

"*Why* did you know it wasn't going to work?"

"He was unstable. Also he drank. When he was doing that he could be mighty cruel."

"You mean like *hit* you?"

"Oh, that, too, but the things he said hurt more."

"Like *what*?"

"I've forgotten. I really have. I need my self-esteem. And he was a sick person, so it wasn't entirely his fault. He was in a mental hospital for servicemen during the war."

"Is he . . . in one now?"

"No, the last I heard he was in Florida, teaching tennis in a hotel."

"Doesn't he ever want to see me?"

"I think he probably does, but, you know, Christina, everyone isn't as *resolute* as we are. Some people can want to do things, but then they don't follow through. Now your Aunt Demaris is the very opposite of your father. She follows through. Which is why I got onto this subject, which isn't my favorite. But I needed to fill you in some before you were exposed to . . . well, other points of view." She was being unusually careful in choosing her words. "When Daddy died suddenly, Demaris and Karl drove up for the funeral in their Cadillac and we'd hardly buried him before Demaris made me a proposition. She wanted me to bring you to live

with them, she wanted to sort of adopt us both.
The offer didn't include Mother. Demaris didn't
like Mother very much. She considered her
'cold'—Mother didn't know how to gush—and
also I think Demaris had Mother's role in mind
for herself. I said I would need some time to
consider it."

"Did you consider it?"

"Not really. Oh, I fantasized some. Obviously
we would have been spoiled to death, but I
would have sacrificed our independence. And
how could I have just deserted my own mother
like that at such a time? But Demaris is the type
of person it's easier to turn down in a letter."

They were down the mountain curves. The
morning sun grew stronger along the straight
road until they could feel its heat inside the car.
"Why, it's plain warm down here in the flat-
lands!" said Christina's mother. She pulled into
a roadside picnic area and they ate their sandwiches in their coats at a table strewn with fallen
leaves and acorn shells. Each time they unscrewed
the top of the Thermos, the hot coffee sent steam

into their cold faces. "Well, isn't this just *grand,*" declared her mother meaningfully, and they both recalled the leopard coat and hat and muff and burst into giggles. The mother breathed in the sharp, clean air and looked around with delight at the deserted picnic grounds and the bare trees. "You know, despite everything, I am glad to have kept my independence. I hope you will feel I did right."

The elderly man by the window offered to trade places with her when he learned that this was to be Christina's first flight. They changed seats and he laughed good-naturedly when he had to keep letting out the seat-belt straps to make ends meet over his portly middle. He sat back in complacent nonchalance as the plane roared and shuddered and raced down the runway past the point of no return and lifted into an emptiness tilting danger-ously to one side and then the other. Christina was grateful to have the example of his calm masculine demeanor. By the time they reached

cruising altitude, the most amazing fictions, re-
plete with realistic details, were pouring out of
her in response to his congenial inquiries. She
was going to spend Christmas with her father,
who owned ranches in Texas and Alabama. Yes,
her mother and father were divorced, had been
since she was a little baby. At first they had been
crazy about each other, but it just didn't work
out.

That happens, he said with an understanding
nod.

Her father insisted on having her every other
Christmas. They would ride around the ranch
on horseback and then go into town and have
lunch and go shopping. Her mother always
worried he would spoil her with all his money,
but she had hopes and dreams of her own, and
besides, she valued her independence.

As they were landing, the man declared feel-
ingly that he would have considered himself
honored by the gods to have been granted a
smart, lovely daughter like herself.

As they disembarked, an elegant, sharp-faced

man in black tie and evening clothes stepped forward at the gate and pronounced her name. For an instant she was confused, it was like walking into her own fantasy. As the man was introducing himself as Clint, who worked for her uncle, she was aware that her traveling companion, a few passengers behind, would assume he was witnessing the father-daughter reunion. What if he should come up to them and say something to expose her? But he passed on discreetly, with a brief nod and a wistful smile.

Close up, Mr. Clint, as he told Christina everyone called him, was not as elegant as his first impression. His face was tough and large-pored, and after he had stored her suitcase in the trunk of the Cadillac and explained that her aunt and uncle were at a dinner party they could not get out of and had sent him to meet her, settle her in at the house, and then go back to pick them up, she decided he must be some kind of upper-grade servant, between a butler and a chauffeur.

But he was a smooth-enough talker without saying or asking much and glibly kept awkwardness at bay.

It was dark by the time they turned into the gates of the ranch, which was named "New Canaan" on Aunt Demaris's stationery, so she couldn't admire the approach, which Mr. Clint boasted was stunning. In daylight from this entrance road you could see a hundred miles in both directions. That would be farther than she and her mother had driven today. But it would be a hundred miles *less* than her mother would have driven on the round trip. For some reason this gave Christina satisfaction.

The house was lit as though the aunt and uncle were having a huge party themselves, but inside there was nobody at home but the maids in their black uniforms and white aprons, only one of whom spoke so-so English. They served Christina her lone supper in the chandeliered dining room: thin slices of steak in a tasty sauce, with yellow rice and some spicy compote and warm tortillas swaddled in white linen on a silver dish, with guacamole and sour cream and a pale green relish heaped attractively in crystal side dishes. She would probably have eaten twice as much if they hadn't been taking turns peeking at her through the tiny hole in the kitchen door. She tried a bite of the mystery relish and choked: she had drunk all the water in her goblet. The maid who didn't speak English burst through the swinging door with a pitcher of water. "Too *caliente*," Christina apologized between gulps. "But it's *muy buena, gracias*. Everything is just *muy buena! LA COMIDA ES MUCHA BUENA.*"

The other maid rushed into the dining room. Standing on either side of her they began chattering eagerly at her in their language. Christina exhausted her meager supply of Spanish phrases convincing them she could not follow. For dessert there was *flan* with caramel sauce, and a small glass of a sweet pinkish wine.

Big and little clocks, distant and close, kept chiming the quarter hours and still they didn't come. Christina felt it would show poor manners to go to her room and lie down, so she chose a tolerably comfortable straight-backed brocade sofa, beneath a life-size oil painting of a platinum blonde Rubenesque lady in a low-cut red gown and red jewels. Feeling more relaxed from the sweet wine, she arranged herself into a portrait of a modest young woman awaiting, not at all resentfully, the return of two *grand* people she had been longing to meet. The Christmas tree in the corner of the living room was loaded with ornaments that had the look of all being bought at the same time. It was bigger and bushier than the one that now took up most of their living room back home, but this room was big enough to dwarf the larger tree. Beneath the tree were piled dozens of professionally wrapped presents, an excessive number of them bearing cards with her name. She wished she had brought gifts, but nobody had been able to come up with any sure idea of what might please the millionaire relatives.

The Texas Christmas tree blinked its colored lights at her. On and off. On and off. They will be getting ready for bed now at home, Christina thought. My grandmother is switching off her last program; my mother reads a couple more paragraphs in her library novel, then sighs and turns down the page. Maybe they are speaking of me at this very moment. Then with a desolate jolt she remembered they were two time zones later than she and by now would be asleep. On and off blinked the lights.

Then there was a sudden brightness and energy, a burst of outdoor air and a fusillade of extravagant welcomes and endearments. The maids fluttered about like two nervous black birds, plucking at the sleek coats of the two large people who stood quite sumptuously still, allowing themselves to be unwrapped for her delight. Christina heard herself called blessed girl and darling one and *much* prettier than her pictures and a great deal more. She was praised exorbitantly for her courtesy in waiting up for them. Now she, too, was standing, offering herself to their hugs and compliments and perfumed kisses. Aunt Demaris was of course the platinum blonde lady in the oil painting, only now she was wearing a black gown and different jewels and had grown much more Rubenesque in figure. But her face was still elegantly planed and beautiful. "We had a *flat tire,* of all things! Would you believe it, darling?"

"Inexcusable is what I say," roared the big rosy uncle. "A brand new automobile just out of the showroom and there we are on the side of a dirt road, me and Mr. Clint, jacking up a blowout in our tuxedos," Despite the mishap he seemed elated.

"He was superb, Christina. Yes, you were, my darling. Mr. Clint wasn't too keen on spoiling *his* finery until your Uncle Karl here set the example. He gave me his cufflinks to hold and rolled up his sleeves and got right down to business in the dirt."

"I hope I haven't forgotten how to change a tire," said the uncle, whose clothes bore no sign of any contact with the dirt. "Well, well, well, Demmie," he exclaimed expansively, an arm around each of them. "We hit the jackpot, didn't we, with this pretty girl here!"

. . .

After another glass of the sweet wine for her and her aunt, and "something stronger" for the uncle, during which there were extensive inquiries about her airplane flight and her dinner and the well-being of her mother and grandmother, whom Aunt Demaris said they must remember to phone first thing in the morning, they sent Christina off to bed. Since she had been to her room last, the maids had unpacked her new suitcase and put everything away where they thought it should go and turned off some lamps and turned on others. Everything looked inviting and pretty, if a little stuffy and overdone. Her folded pajamas awaited her on the pillow, her cosmetics and brush and comb were laid out across the glass top of the vanity. She hung up her dress and got into her pajamas and rinsed out her stockings, panties, and garter belt in the adjoining bathroom. She had just arranged them on the towel rack next to the sink and was drying off her hands when there was a soft knock at the bedroom door.

The maids had unpacked her new suitcase and put everything away

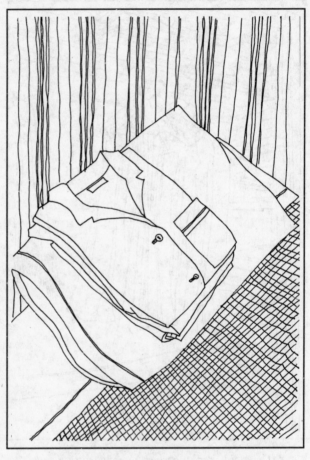

Her folded pajamas awaited her on the pillow

"I simply had to see my girl one more time," said her aunt, sweeping in. "Ah, you're already in your dear pajamas. Are these flannel? We might want to get you something lighter while you're in Texas." Demaris had changed into a creamy satin kimono with braided gold loops down the bosom. Her face, cleaned of its makeup and lubricated for the night with an orange-smelling cream, made her seem simpler and more open.

"Come sit here by me on the bed and let me look at you." Which she proceeded to do in minuscule detail. Face, hair, nose, eyes, figure, were described and praised in turn. Then she stroked Christine's hands and pulled at the corners, proclaiming them to be exact replicas of her grandfather's. "Uncle Tommy had the same sweet hands, small for a man's, but strong—he worked in the iron mines when he was young, you know. He was the world's kindest man. I wish you could have known him!"

Christina said she wished she could have, too, adding that her mother and grandmother still spoke of him most every day.

"Not a *single* day goes by that *I* don't think of him," rejoined her aunt passionately, making Christina feel she had betrayed them at home by not exaggerating and saying every single day.

Aunt Demaris strolled into Christina's bathroom and stood gazing pensively down into the toilet bowl, as if hoping to read clues to her niece's character. Thank God she had flushed. Then she saw her aunt stiffen when she discovered the wet stockings, panties, and garter belt on the towel rack next to the sink. "Ah, darling," she scolded sadly. "We can't have you doing the *washing* here. We'll let it go this time, but from now on just put your little things in this net bag behind the bathroom door and Marta will take care of them for you."

Christina had not failed to notice the baby blue rosary draped invitingly across the small, framed wedding picture on her bedside table. A young, slim, rather fierce-looking bride clung proudly to the arm of her butcher boy husband. As it

"Ah, darling, we can't have you doing the washing here."

happened, Christina was acquainted with the mysteries of the rosary, as well as its soporific effects. But she had no desire to disturb it from its ornamental function tonight and presently consigned the whole room and its contents, as well as those of the adjoining bathroom, into pitch darkness. She arranged her limbs straight as a mummy's between the soft Marta-laundered sheets and simply breathed in and out until she could feel the return of her own spirit come like a sudden rush of oxygen to her lungs. Scenes she had no control of, based on nothing she had seen during this eventful day, surged toward her on the inside of her eyelids, then rapidly gave way to other scenes. As she lay there calming down she rightly guessed that she would make many stupid mistakes before the end of her visit, and that she would be forgiven each time, perhaps even loved more for them. They would be discussed as touching and charming and a little sad after she was gone.

Already she knew deep down in a part of herself she had yet to meet, that these people

were not for her. But there would be future opportunities for temptation, and one or two times
just short of desperation, when she would do
her level best to surrender herself into their cap-
tive embrace. But each time, by the grace of
God, wherever he operates from, and thanks to
the independence her mother had early ruined
her with, she would sabotage herself and blight
her chances, again and again, with these grand
people so eager to make life easy for her.

Old Lovegood Girls

In the latest Lovegood College Alumnae Bulletin, I see that Mrs. Elizabeth Mc-Corkle Snyder has given a memorial donation "in memory of Miss Carol Olafson, formerly P.E. and Health teacher." I don't recall Miss Mc-Corkle (she was a spinster in those days) being a particular friend of our easygoing, tomboyish gym teacher, but perhaps she was made solemn—as I always am—by the finality of death: especially when it claims someone you have known. Also, knowing Miss McCorkle, I suspect she regards her donation as one more obstinate stone added to the fortress of memory. Memory, as she repeatedly instructed us, was our best defense against the barbaric forces that periodically try to trample down our gates and make rubbish of our glorious achievements.

Miss McCorkle herself was the very opposite of easygoing. One girl in our class had hysterics and had to go to the infirmary because she couldn't memorize all the countries belonging to the British Crown in the year of Queen Victoria's jubilee for Miss McCorkle's test the next day; and I still catch myself murmuring "... Antietam ... Fredericksburg ... Chancellorsville ... Gettysburg ..." at the oddest moments.

Last year I had to fly around the country a lot, and on one of my flights I sat next to a brittle, stylish woman whose business, she told me, was designing brochures for colleges to send out to prospective students. First she would visit the

Lovegood College

college and prowl around the campus for several weeks, she said; she would seek out old alumnae, ask around town for people's impressions of the college—people who could be objective in their impressions; and then she would go back home to her drawing board and come up with an "image" of the college that could be suitably captured in a brochure.

"I've just returned from this junior college in North Carolina that you wouldn't believe," she told me. "In this day and time it's an anachronism, that's what it is. The girls there . . . well, they're still *girls,* for one thing: they think of themselves as girls. And they're good girls; they walk around that beautiful campus looking too good to be true. I wouldn't be surprised if many of them were still virgins. No, I'm not kidding. This school is a hotbed of all the old virtues: you know, duty, loyalty, charity, respect for all the old traditions of religion and society. The place is actually called Lovegood College. 'Love good.' And you should see their graduation ceremony, I was there for it. The 'girls' wear white, off-the-shoulder ball gowns, with hoops, and each girl carries two dozen long-stemmed roses. It's in the evening, and after they get their diplomas, they go out to the fountain in front of this gigantic old antebellum mansion with columns four stories high, and each 'girl' throws one dozen roses into the fountain. Then she hands over her second bunch to her *mother*—or some aunt or godmother if the mother is dead—and the mother graciously takes out one single rose and gives it back to the daughter. That's all she gets to keep for herself, the Lovegood 'girl': one rose. At the end of the ceremony, the pool around the fountain is clogged with roses."

"Really?" I said.

"Yes. It's all very symbolic." The stylish woman rolled her eyes and gave a little smirk of contempt. "The roses in the fountain mean she leaves part of herself at the school, consecrates herself to its purposes. And after she pays her dues to Mother—and all *that* stands for—she's got one rose to show for herself. You don't know how many dried roses were proudly displayed to me when I visited the homes of alumnae and had coffee—never anything stronger. Always served out of trousseau china cups in cozy kitchens decorated with Ethan Allen furniture. The really amazing thing is: the college is rolling in money, and most of it comes from old alumnae. It has endowments coming out its ears. It can buy the latest computers for its business students. It can send novice missionaries—it's a Presbyterian school—to Japan for a 'trial run' semester. It's all very strange." She seemed momentarily baffled by this unfashionable combination of virtue and money.

"You don't sound as though you liked the place very much," I said. "How will you design the brochure?"

"Oh, my dear, that's easy!" Her eyes gleamed with triumphant irony as she touched the sleeve of my jacket. "On the cover will be . . . just a single, long-stemmed red rose . . . with a drop of dew on it. They'll love it!"

After I got off the plane I wondered why I hadn't let her have it. What had held me back? My Lovegood charity? My Southern-bred disdain for people who started angry scenes? Or was I not just a little intimidated by her fashion-able worldly cynicism? Do modern barbarians pose as cynics, slipping stylishly through our gates, while we—fearing their ridicule—hesitate and are lost?

My father and I told everybody that the reason we had chosen Lovegood College for me was because it was the first college we visited, during that sweltering July weekend, where the president gave us lemonade and invited my father to take off his jacket. There were other factors, of course, but we left them out in the interest of a better story.

Actually, there were three colleges on our list. All were located in the state capital, a city twenty-five miles from the tiny tobacco-growing town where my father lived. As I was new to my father, and he to me, we wanted me to be near enough so that I could spend frequent weekends with him.

Our first choice had been St. Mark's College.

Not only had I been raised an Episcopalian by my mother, but this college had a reputation as being the classiest of the three. Our first interview was there, but the rector's reserve inhibited my father's spontaneity and put us both on the defensive. The rector politely inquired why we had left things until so late: most incoming freshmen had applied the previous year. "My daughter has just come to live with me," said my father, refusing to elaborate, and I'm sure we both gave the impression, stifled as we were by the inhospitable surroundings, of having something to hide. Nevertheless the rector said a place *might* be found for me—assuming of course that my transcript grades were what I said they were—and the way we left it was that my father would call him on Monday morning and let him know our decision.

As we walked to the parking lot, my father said, "I don't know about you, but as far as I'm concerned he can wait for my call until hell freezes over."

"I feel the same," I said.

We got into the black-and-white Mercury Montclair demonstrator that my father liked because it matched his black-and-white French Shriner shoes, and he started the motor and turned the air conditioner on high. "The Baptist college comes next on the list," he said. "Are we sure we want a Baptist college? The Baptists can be so fanatical about alcohol."

"Maybe not, then," I said. We were on our father-daughter honeymoon, so to speak, and I wished to agree with him in all things. Baptists didn't move me strongly one way or the other.

So we bypassed the Baptist college, my father stopping at a pay phone to cancel the appointment, and then we drove in a leisurely, meandering way toward the older section of the city so we would not be too early for our appointment at the Presbyterian college. At last we descended a hilly street full of Victorian houses sinking into genteel decay, and, halfway down this street, the buxom four-story

Doric columns of Lovegood loomed impressively into view.

"Now that must have been some place to live," said my father. We both knew already that I was going to live there.

If I failed to notice any striking want of rebelliousness in Lovegood girls during my first weeks at the school, it was probably because I was too busy being grateful and good myself. I was happy to be at Lovegood. The haven of security and propriety it offered was just what I needed. I was still panting hard from my close brush with downward mobility: last spring, I had abandoned hope of being at *any* college in the fall. My stepfather, still uncertain in his profession, did not yet make the kind of money that could send someone off to college without them helping; to add to his difficulties, there was now his own baby girl and another baby on the way. The two scholarships I had tried for had fallen through, and, in a late-spring period of vindictive despair, I had engaged myself to an air force man my mother thought wasn't good enough. I really do not know what I might have done (or not done) with my life if my father had not made his timely and dramatic appearance at my high school graduation. I had sent him an invitation as a sort of bitter jest: I had not laid eyes on him since I was a child—and then only briefly, on two short occasions.

But as fate would have it—and I don't use the word lightly—the invitation reached him at the very time when he was doing a little bookkeeping: adding up the debits and credits of his life. He was forty-nine years old, and all he had to show for his efforts were a shelf full of tennis trophies, a modest brick bungalow that he had bought with what was left of his inheritance from his mother, and a small sum of money he had been able to put away during the last two years, because he had managed to stay off the bottle and take advantage of a booming automobile market. When my invitation arrived, it struck him suddenly that I might be a credit to him. I mean, in another sense besides being a tax-deductible dependent. He had been illegally claiming me as *that* for many years, he later confessed to me, in one of his wry, dark, self-deprecatory moments.

On the morning of my graduation day, he put on his white suit, drove his favorite demonstrator across town to pick up his brother the judge, also wearing his white suit, and then their sister Edie; then he doubled back to his side of town, to his boss's house, to pick up a young widow named Myrna—the boss's sister-in-law and my father's girlfriend, who hadn't been ready the first time he came by—and off they started, for a public high school two hundred miles away. Because of Myrna's dilatory toilette, they missed half of my salutatory address. I had no idea they were there until after the diplomas had been handed out and my father came up to me in the hall and introduced himself. Having kept an outdated picture of him in my head, I didn't recognize him at first. Then there was a brief, awkward meeting with my mother, who was seven months pregnant with my stepfather's second child, and after that I went out to a Howard Johnson's in the demonstrator with my new family. I was impressed with them: all three were large, handsome people with rich, authoritative, rather sarcastic voices. They teased one another a lot. My widowed aunt courted me in her dry, egocentric way, firing questions at me and insisting that I had my father's features; my uncle kept saying to the table at large, "Isn't she pretty . . . isn't she pretty"; with his thick thatch of gray hair and his air of benevolent gloom, he became exactly my image of how a Southern judge should be. My father was still very handsome, though he had filled out a lot, and I could see why he had taken the route of least resistance and been a playboy as long as he could. That evening I even thought Myrna was sweet. She was a lisping, fadingly pretty woman with a neat, full figure. She seemed in awe of me and laughed hilariously at the constant sarcastic banter of the other three.

"How about spending the summer with me?" my father said. "Or have you made other plans?"

I said I'd love to spend the summer with him.

"Where are you going to college?" demanded my aunt.

"I may not be going," I said.

"Not going to college!" exclaimed my uncle. "A smart girl like you."

I explained my stepfather's predicament. "So I may have to work a year first."

"We'll see about that," said my father. Shyly, he squeezed my hand under the table.

Lovegood College put on a memorable Orientation Pageant, which took place in the school chapel. Its purpose was obviously to enamor newcomers of its traditions and knit us solidly into the community. New girls were seated in the front pews. Then the lights went out, the music teacher struck up "Lead On, O King Eternal," the Lovegood processional hymn, on the big pipe organ, and the old girls, carrying lighted candles, marched in twos up the center aisle, singing the fervent hymn. They divided into single file at the front and returned down the two side aisles to take their seats behind us. They had seen the pageant before.

First came the history of Lovegood, written and directed by the energetic Miss Elizabeth Mc-Corkle. We had heard about this pageant: the history teacher always organized it the previous spring and handed out the parts to her favorite girls so they could memorize them over the summer. First came scenes depicting the grand life as it had been lived in this building during the golden antebellum days, when Lovegood was the proud plantation home of Horace Lanier Lovegood and his family and faithful slaves. Then came the darker scenes, when war raged and Lovegoods hid the silver and prayed for their absent loved ones in battle. Then came the scene in which the mansion was turned into a Confederate hospital and Lovegood daughters covered their curls with nurses' caps and tended the wounded. Finally came the stirring scene in which the enlightened Presbyterian educator, Dr. Manley Phipps, purchased the decaying Lovegood from the last living member of the clan, a gracious old lady in her eighties, who says, "I hope that future generations of Lovegood girls will be as happy and as carefree as I was in that house." Dr. Phipps was played with great dash by Miss McCorkle herself, wearing a top hat, striped trousers, and morning coat. The doddering Lovegood daughter was portrayed very realistically by one of my roommates, a sophomore named Hermione Broadstead, who, at nineteen, had an uncanny old-ladyish air about her, even when her brown hair was not powdered white and she wore her everyday saddle oxfords, sweater sets, and pearls.

After the history pageant, there was another hymn, and the presidents of the various student organizations got up and advertised their activities. The most esteemed of these organizations were the Lovegood Daughters and Granddaughters Club (for which I was not eligible, as neither my mother nor grandmother had gone to Lovegood) and the Lovegood Christian Association, for which no girl was eligible until she had proved her spiritual and intellectual worthiness for an entire semester. Not only must she maintain at least a 3.5 average in all subjects, but her moral character must be voted "outstanding" by a unanimous committee of faculty and peers. As the current president of the association related these stiff requirements in a sugary eastern Carolina drawl, I remember thinking her distinctly priggish. But I squashed the thought at once, because I decided I would try to get into this select organization: how proud it would make my father.

The final number on the program was a poetry reading by our English teacher. A tall, mournfully beautiful woman, she mounted the platform, her narrow ankles teetering slightly in her high-heeled pumps. Fingering the brooch at the throat of her lacy, high-necked blouse, she explained to us in a voice that sounded as if she were either on the verge of tears or of some great emotion that the long poem she was about to read had been written by one of the state's renowned poets of the last century after a stay at

Lovegood Plantation. "It was not uncommon, in those days, for a houseguest to write a poem about his host's home, if he had enjoyed a particularly happy stay there—and especially," the ghost of a smile lit up her pale, classic features, "if the houseguest happened to be a poet."

Then Miss Petrie—her first name was Fiona—read to us "The Melodies of Lovegood Plantation: Spring, 1851." The poem would not have survived the scornful hearing of the brochure-woman on the airplane for a minute, but read as it was in Miss Petrie's throaty, melancholy voice that reminded one of a cello, it could make the willing listener enter a kind of dream. Whatever narrowness or effusions the poem manifested, Fiona Petrie's reading of it made you long for some lost birthright of an irrecoverable past both glorious and innocent. I knew all about Miss Petrie through the student grapevine, which provided its own very effective form of orientation: from an impeccably old family in Beaufort, she had been the flower of her year when she had been presented in this

very city, at some terpsichorean ball before
World War II. Then she had gone away to college in Virginia, and something had happened:
either a lover had been killed in the war, or married another—the grapevine wasn't sure—and
after that, Miss Petrie stopped going out with
men altogether. Now she and Miss Olafson, the
pert, grinning gym teacher from somewhere in
the Midwest, shared an apartment off-campus,
driving to and from school each day in Miss
Olafson's Jeep. Miss Petrie herself did not drive.

As I sat there under the spell of her voice,
watching her delicate white fingers flutter occa-
sionally to her throat, or brush away a curl of her
short, dark hair, it suddenly occurred to me that
what my father needed in his life was an elegant
woman like this. He had me, of course, and he
had told me several times during our summer
idyll that I was "the first thing worth being good
for" that he had found in a long time. But I
couldn't *always* be there, and I had seen enough
of his life in that dull little town to understand
the opportunities for despair and dissolution it

offered to someone of my father's temperament who happened to be stuck there. It was all right for his brother, whose profession gave him status and power and backslapping lunches with hearty lawyers and businessmen, not to mention the stagelike gratification of being always the calm character of authority who held sway over messier, violent lives. But what about my father, driving down dusty country roads in search of a farmer ready to trade up on a new Lincoln? What thoughts did he have? What regrets? What painful memories of unaccomplished dreams? He had confided in me, during a week we had spent at his boss's cottage at Carolina Beach, that he regretted not having made more of himself, and told me I mustn't let it happen to me. But, in a more upbeat tone, later, as we were lying together on the beach, working on our tans, he had told me I was his good angel, and that if he continued to win his battle against depression and alcohol, and if automobile sales continued like this, well, the future might not be so hopeless after all. Since that conversation, I had tried to picture a suitable future for my father, but, try as I would, I couldn't get him out of that town. Where would he go? Except for those dilettante winters spent in Florida teaching tennis, after he and my mother divorced, he had always lived in this town. And, if he weren't "Manager of Sales" at the W. O. Creech Lincoln-Mercury Agency, what would he be doing?

The other problem I had in trying to imagine a future for him was keeping Myrna out of it. He saw her almost every night. (Who else, in that town, was there for him to see? All the women his age were long married; some were grandmothers.) She was his boss's sister-in-law, and he had told me himself that "W. O." was getting impatient for Myrna to find a new life for herself so that he could turn his garage apartment back into a rental property. My father was a dead ringer for Myrna's next husband. I knew they were physically intimate from the way they touched each other and played around, although—out of some paternal fastidiousness—he always went to Myrna's garage apartment when I was sleeping at his house. I would hear him trying to let himself in quietly when he came home around four AM.

Myrna had been nice to me, she had even tried to "win" me, in her uncertain, affected way, inviting me for little lunches in her apartment, consulting gravely with me, as gravely as her lisp would allow, over what kind of clothes a girl should take to college. I wished I could like her better, but there was something a little common about her. It was my belief that my father needed a higher sort of being, someone else "worth being good for" if he were to survive in that dusty little town. He needed a second angel in the house on whom he could depend to take over his happiness after I had gone out into the world in pursuit of mine.

If you want a saint, go to Lovegood;
If you want good lovin', go to St. Mark's.

In this way, the boys at State, Duke, and Chapel Hill summed up their dating experiences at two of the three women's colleges in the capital city. There was another jingle that included all three colleges. The first two lines are too obscene to print, but the third line was:

and Love *Good girls.*

Even in salacious college-boy doggerel, we came out unscathed.

I knew, even in those first "good and grateful" weeks, that I was not completely a Lovegood girl. My nature was too restless and experimental to accept without question Lovegood's definitions of womanly worth, to pledge myself—before conducting some experiments of my own—to conserving its standards. Also, by the standards of those doggerel verses, I had forfeited my "sainthood" the previous spring with my air force man, forfeited it deliberately and vehemently: if I was going to have to go straight from high school to adulthood, I had told myself, why should I not start enjoying at once the pleasures of adulthood?

But then my father had entered the picture

and changed everything: I was to have a few more blessed years of carefree youth, after all. I was sorry I had committed myself so precipitately to the air force man, but then, during the summer, things had resolved themselves fortuitously, after all. My intended wrote from his base in Seattle to confess that he had gotten a girl in trouble and had to marry her. While my father was at work, I rode his bicycle down to the post office and mailed off an engagement ring he had never known I had. I remember thinking as I pedaled home, past the rose gardens of all the sleepy houses with their curtains drawn against the heat, how fortunate I was not to have been that girl who got "caught."

So, if those first weeks at Lovegood I felt I was in some sense playacting the ingénue, it was a role whose safety and simplicity refreshed and soothed me as I tucked in the corners of my Bates bedspread every morning and arranged my stuffed animals on top; as I went out with a Lambda Chi from State and wouldn't let him touch me for the first three dates; as I sat in the balcony of the civic auditorium, partaking of the operas and concerts that were included in the price of my tuition; as I walked uptown to church on Sundays in the bloc of Lovegood girls, all of us wearing white gloves and little pillbox hats with wisps of veils. It was as if I were monitoring myself—or, rather, as if the old me watched a diligent, privileged, and thankful new self—as I hunched under the green-shaded lamps at the long table in the library and memorized for Dr. Fellowes, our Bible teacher, the names of the Children of Israel who went into Egypt; memorized in chronological order the battles of the War between the States for Miss McCorkle, until the night watchman, a frightening-looking grizzled old man with a limp, whom someone had nicknamed Old Orlick, came shuffling down the rows of books, jingling his keys at us late studiers so he could lock up the library at ten.

Lights-out was at ten thirty on weeknights, though we were allowed to play our radios very softly until eleven. There was a program called

"My Best to You," on which songs were played for various Lovegood or St. Mark's or Sheridan College girls from their boyfriends at State. Sometimes the disc jockey, whose older, mellow voice reminded me a little of my father's, would read sad, nostalgic poetry over the air, and my roommate, Hermione Broadstead, who loved sad, nostalgic things, would weep softly in the dark.

"I was down in Pine Level this week, showing a rich tobacco farmer the new Lincoln," said my father, as he drove me home with him one bright October weekend. "When I told him I had a daughter at Lovegood, he said he'd tried like anything to get his daughter to go there, but she wasn't having any. She told him she wasn't about to be shut up in a convent. I told him *you* seemed happy. Is it like a convent? I hope you don't think I railroaded you into going there. I honestly didn't know it was stricter than the other colleges. Is it?"

"A little," I said. "I mean, we're the only girls who have to be in by eleven on Saturday nights.

And we can't even date during the week until our sophomore year. But I don't mind it. In the first place, there's no one I'm mad to date, and in the second place, I'm enjoying concentrating on my work."

"It's nice to hear that," my father said.

"I don't think that man's daughter just meant the rules," I said. "There's something else about Lovegood. It's hard to explain. It's like . . . well, there's this *tradition* you have to uphold. I mean, you realize it's all a little outdated, but yet . . . but yet *you* don't want to be the one to break this tradition." Then, by way of explaining further, I quoted to him the repeatable one of the two college-boy slogans.

My father laughed. "And do you mind being a saint?"

I considered this for a minute, knowing what he was really asking. "I don't know if I'm a saint or not," I said at last, "but, well . . . I like *trying* to be one."

He seemed quite satisfied with my answer. We drove for a while through tobacco country without speaking. The harvests of the summer were already drying in barns, or being turned into cigarettes, and the fields had been plowed under to wait for the next planting in the spring.

Then my father said, rather shyly, "I'm *glad,* you know, that . . . well, how shall I say it? I'm glad I found you while you were still fresh and unspoiled by life."

In the evenings after supper, at Lovegood, my other roommate, a sophomore named Laura Jean Fletcher, who was already engaged to an agricultural major at State, would put the lid up on the grand piano in the parlor and play for us until evening study hall began. She was an emotional pianist, liberal with the loud pedal, caring more for throbbing chords and arpeggios than for a hundred-percent score of right notes; but she could play just about every well-known tune anybody could ask for. Hermione always asked for "When I Grow Too Old to Dream," and sometimes wept appreciatively while it was be-ing played.

During these sessions at the piano, I would often slip out of the room and climb the wide stairs to the fourth floor of the old building and go out on its top porch. Leaning my cheek against one of its mammoth, cool, white columns, I would look down at the soft night spread out before me and imagine I was in the last century. I would imagine I was one of the daughters of the household, rich and docile and protected, perfectly patient to wait up there—while piano music rippled gaily from a lower floor—until the man who would be good enough for me, perhaps even better, would ride up the curving driveway, its white pebbles gleaming under starlight, and enter the house and ask my father for my hand. On other evenings, feeling more pragmatic, I would stand up there seeing how many buildings I could recognize from their distant lights up on the capital's hill, or I would inhale deep drafts of the mellow, Southern fall air, and imagine myself rich and famous in some future life.

. . .

The more I saw of Fiona Petrie, the more I admired her. She would be just the right woman for my father. As I relaxed in the gentle oasis of her English hour, after the grim long marches of memorization and feedback in Bible and history, I scrutinized her covertly while she read aloud to us in her cello-voice from *Paradise Lost*. I judged her to be somewhere in her early forties. She was a little too thin, but her structure was long-boned and feminine. Her face, though no longer blooming with youth, would retain its classic lines until she died. There was some silver in her crisp, black, curly hair, but it made her look distinguished. It would go well with the silver in my father's hair. And I loved the way she dressed: her dignified, well-cut skirts that floated as she walked; her large variety of old-fashioned blouses; her brooch, her cameo, and her pearls. What a contrast to Myrna's bright frocks with their revealing contours. But it was her voice that charmed me most, accompanied by certain poignant expressions that would flit, from time to time, across her face, as she read lines such as:

From morn
To noon he fell, from noon to dewy eve

or:

Thick as autumnal leaves that strow the brooks
In Vallombrosa.

I worked hard in her class to become a favorite, but it was the type of work that came easy to me. I could memorize, if I had to, all the countries of the British Commonwealth in the days when the sun never set on it, and I had become quite adept at ferreting out the obscure kind of fact that Dr. Fellowes loved to spring on his quizzes. (Q. How tall was Goliath? A. Six cubits and a span. I Samuel, 17.4.) But it was much more compatible for me to be asked to write long, thoughtful essays on philosophical problems, or short stories with "epiphanies."

Not only did I take great pains to shape my

sentences so that they would be appealing as well as correct, but I cunningly chose subjects that would reveal to her aspects of myself—and of the man whom she might one day marry. And so far, things had gone well. "This moved me very much," she wrote on my short story about a girl and her father lying on the beach, discussing how thankful they were to have been reunited. In the last line of the story, the handsome father murmurs against the sound of the waves: "Now I feel I have something to be good for again."

The weather stayed mild into early November, and Miss Petrie and Miss Olafson would often eat their bagged lunches on the sunny steps outside the gym, so that Miss Olafson could stay in her sweat suit. After lunch in our communal dining room, where girls sat eight to a round table and rotated every other week, "so we would get to know everybody," I would often join the two teachers outside, as they dawdled over their final carrot sticks or fruit. They always seemed pleased to have me join them, and I was pretty sure Miss Petrie must have said nice things about me to her friend, because Miss Olafson put herself out to make herself agreeable to me, asking me all sorts of questions about myself (many of which she could not have asked had she not known something of the content of my essays and short stories) and grinning to herself when I answered, as if she found my replies clever and amusing. A small, wiry woman with several dark moles on her face, she had none of Miss Petrie's elegance or beauty, but her easygoing, joking, informal manner was an attractive contrast. And she seemed to be good for Miss Petrie. As she sat there peeling the apple or sectioning the tangerine they always shared, she would tease "Fiona" for not being able to drive or play tennis. Miss Petrie would utter a short, exhausted laugh as if it were being torn from her and say, "Oh, Carol, I'm not coordinated and never will be." But the English teacher's face would glow for a moment with just a hint of color, and she would smile faintly as her hands fluttered down to tuck her skirt around her knees. When they were married, I thought, my father would teach her to laugh—though she would never be capable of Myrna's unrestrained giggles. I could already picture him teaching her to play tennis, standing behind her and putting his hands on top of hers on the racket. At night, even when they got old, they would lie in bed, perhaps in some beach cottage near the sound of the waves, and she would read to him about the thick autumnal leaves and the brooks of Vallombrosa. The next thing that had to happen, of course, was for him to meet her, but first I wanted to prepare him for her as I had been preparing her—through my stories and casually scattered references—for him. During the Thanksgiving break I would begin to speak to him of Fiona Petrie, and, sometime before Christmas, I would arrange a meeting: maybe a "conference" they could have, about me.

My father was not in a good mood when he came in the demonstrator to pick me up for the

Thanksgiving weekend. It was the first time he had been so preoccupied and restrained around me, and I wasn't sure how to behave. I didn't yet know him well enough to know whether he liked to be jollied out of his bad moods, or asked what was the matter, or whether he was the kind of man who would rather you act as if you had noticed nothing unusual. I made pallid attempts at conversation, telling him how the whole Sigma Chi fraternity had come over to Lovegood College and stood in the driveway in front of the fountain and sung to all the girls who stood looking down on them from the three balconies, which seemed to amuse him some—at least it drew from him a dry smile; but I didn't risk describing the charms of Fiona Petrie, as I had planned to on this very drive. I had learned enough about men from my mother to know that if you brought up things you wanted when they were in bad moods, they sometimes took offense at these things forever after, and you had destroyed your chances by not waiting for a more opportune moment to present your case.

I was disappointed to find we were having dinner with Myrna—my father usually saved the first night for me—but it turned out not to be so bad, since she and I could make friendly chatter and render his morose silences less ominous. When she and I went to the ladies together, while he was settling the bill, I asked her if she knew what was wrong. We were both lipstick-ing our mouths at the mirror and our eyes met, and her eyelashes trembled and she looked as though she was going to tell me something. But then she only said, "Oh, honey, he gets like that once in a blue moon. If I were you, I'd just be real sweet and gentle with him, and it'll pass."

He seemed in a somewhat better disposition the next morning, although he couldn't have gotten much sleep: I had heard him let himself in at five AM. We went to my widowed Aunt Edie's for the big Thanksgiving meal in the middle of the day. It was not very cold, but overcast and gloomy, and when we arrived we found her arguing with her other brother whether it was cold enough to build a fire. "A fire is more hospitable," said the judge. "Well, if my hospitality's not enough for you, I guess you'd better build one, then," she retorted. They bickered in this fashion even after the fire was built, and on through the meal, but I knew them well enough by now to understand this was their lifelong way of getting along. My father laughed at them, and pretended at several times to play the peacemaker between these spirited, sarcastic, older siblings, and, around three o'clock, we all parted: the judge to go back to his house and take a nap, my father and I expressing our intention to do likewise, and Aunt Edie—as she brusquely announced—to clean up the mess, even though she had refused to let us stay and help her.

When we got back to my father's house, he excused himself to take his nap, and I tried to sleep, but found I couldn't, so I propped up the bed pillows and decided to read ahead in the

Bible—we were up to Job, now—and make lists of potential "pop" questions Dr. Fellowes might spring.

I had been at this task for some time when a shuffly sound made me look up from my concentration. My father was standing in the doorway, with his arms crossed, looking down at me.

"Well, well," he said. "My little daughter in bed, reading the Bible." His voice was slurry and his eyes glittered at me in an unfriendly manner.

"Did you have your nap?" I asked gently, remembering Myrna's advice.

"Not really," he said. "I had too much on my mind."

"Would you . . . would you like to talk about it?" I closed the Bible and moved my notebook out of the way, so he could sit down on the bed if he liked.

But instead, he went over to the bureau and opened the top drawer. He rummaged around among my handkerchiefs and some stockings and things I had left from the summer. He drew out a packet of air mail letters with a ribbon around them. "Did you know you left these here?" he asked.

They were the letters from my ex-fiancé, the air force man. When I had come to live with my father I had brought the letters, just as I had brought the engagement ring in its little velvet box. At the time I hadn't made up my mind what to do: I told myself I still loved the air force man, but I didn't want to ruin my chances with my father, so I hadn't said anything about being engaged. A few more letters had reached me at my father's, but I had always told him they were from some boy I had dated who had since gone into the air force. When I had sent back the ring at the end of the summer, after my fiancé notified me of his sudden necessity to marry the other girl, I had considered making an emotional bonfire of the letters one afternoon when I was in this house alone. Oh, why hadn't I? Why hadn't I?

"I found them most enlightening," my father went on, not expecting me to answer. He probably had all the answer he needed from my face.

"You don't mean to say . . ." I tried the feeble defense of moral outrage, ". . . you don't mean you read my letters."

" 'You *don't* mean you *read* my *letters,*' " echoed my father in a singsong, falsetto voice.

"Well, I'm just shocked," I said, sincerely this time. I was shocked. I had never seen him look at me in such a way. Also, now I recognized the unfamiliar new odor that had come into the room with him. It shocked me that he had broken his proud promise to himself, and that, since he was standing there with those letters in his hand, it might have something to do with me.

"If you think you're shocked, you can imagine what I felt," he said. "No, my dear, I was the one who was shocked. These intimate details . . ." He extricated one of the letters from the pack and with a grimace of disdain let it drop to the rug. "So tasteless . . ." Another letter was dispatched to the floor. "It made me wonder what sort of disgusting things you wrote in yours."

"Well, if I had known you were going to go sneaking around in my drawers, I would have kept carbon copies," I said in a cold voice. "Then you could really have enjoyed yourself." I felt frightened and sick at heart, but also very angry.

"No," he replied quietly, all the nastiness suddenly gone from his tone. "No, I wouldn't have enjoyed myself." He looked down at the remaining letters, as though they had been something dirty he had just discovered in his hand, and put them on top of the bureau. "I don't make a habit of snooping through people's private things," he went on, in a dangerously gentle way, "but, if you want to know the truth, I was lying here last week worrying about business . . . sales are in a slump . . . and wondering what it was all for . . . all the effort of being obliging and charming to perfect strangers so they just might buy an automobile from you . . . and then I thought of you, happy and safe in that school, and I missed you. I was suddenly amazed by my good luck. 'You really have this lovely daughter,' I told myself. 'She really exists. She's your own flesh and blood, and exactly the kind of daughter you would have picked out of a whole lineup of women. And she seems to like you, too.' It made it all worthwhile again. And then I thought I'd like to have something of yours near me, to touch something you had touched. So I came in here and opened that drawer, thinking I'd maybe take one of your pretty handkerchiefs, and that's when I found those. The odd thing was that, the minute I laid eyes on them, I knew the kind of things I'd find inside. I've written a few letters to women in my time. I knew it would be better not to open them, but by that time I couldn't stop myself. It's just like that bottle in there. I know once I break the seal I'm a goner, but when a certain point is reached, there's no going back. What are you crying for? You have nothing to cry about. You have your whole life ahead of you. Think of all the Bible reading you can do." The sarcasm had crept back into his voice, rich and deadly. "Think of all the *other* things

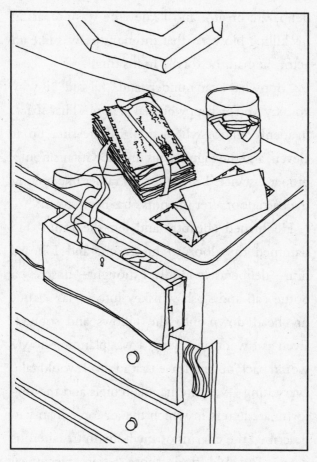

"So I came in here and opened that drawer"

you can do." His eyes shone and he took a deep, deliberate breath, and I knew he was preparing his killing blow. At that moment he was like an actor, he had me totally in his thrall.

"But what I can't understand," he said, "is why you say you're happy at that school. That strict, maidenly school where the girls are shut up at eleven, and the Sigma Chis sing downstairs from a proper distance. I mean, isn't it rather like bolting the barn door after the horse has been stolen?"

He turned abruptly and left the room. He slammed the door to his room, and I heard him—deliberately loudly, I thought—unscrew a bottle cap and slosh whiskey into a glass. I put my head down into the pillows and sobbed. Even as I went on crying, I was planning how I would pack up and leave that night. I would take everything—yes, the handkerchiefs and the unfortunate letters in which the air force man had described the charms of my body in treacherous detail. I would flush those letters piecemeal down one of the powerful Lovegood toilets, which is what I should have done in the first place.

In a few minutes, my father was back. He stood over me, arms dangling at his sides, tears running down his face.

"Can you ever forgive me? You're all I have."

"You're all *I* have."

"No, that's not true," he said sadly. "You have your mother. You'd be in a sorry mess if all you had to depend on in this world was me."

"That's not true. You've changed my life. You made *me* have something worth being good for."

"You're good enough as you are. You're a perfectly normal, healthy young woman. I don't know what I expected. That rotgut puts terrible words in my mouth."

"Don't drink anymore."

"I won't. I stayed off it for two years. Come watch me pour it down the drain."

"And I'll destroy those awful letters," I said magnanimously, leaping up from the bed.

But he dismissed this idea with a weary wave

of his hand and, suddenly looking ill, staggered from the room. Presently I heard him retching in the bathroom. The toilet flushed several times, and then he came out and went to his room. He slept for several hours, during which time I tore the letters quietly into small pieces and stuffed them into a side pocket of my suit-case. I certainly did not want to risk stopping up his toilet with them.

Later that evening, we drove out to a diner on the highway and had sandwiches and coffee. He had wet-combed his hair, and it lay flat on his head, giving him a chastened look. As he sor-rowfully stirred his coffee, he looked up at me from time to time with a wry, sheepish smile. His breath now reeked of Listerine.

"You look as though you'd just lost your last friend," I said, trying to cheer him up.

"I probably have," he replied.

We were tender and careful with each other the rest of the weekend. But we both knew our father-daughter idyll would never be quite the same.

. . .

"It seems to me there are two kinds of goodness in this world," I wrote in my end-of-term essay for Miss Petrie. *"There is the docile, innocent kind that comes from never having tasted the apple, never having had any hardship or challenge, in your safe paradise, to even tempt you to want to taste it. And then there is another kind— far more difficult and admirable, in my opinion—that evolves out of a person's individual experience. A person lives, learns, fails, makes errors and foolish mistakes, even sins: But I do not think this necessarily means that that person is 'defaced, deflowered,' and cursed to death, as Adam tells Eve she is (Bk.IX, PL) before he, too, tastes the fruit. On the contrary, this person might determine all the harder to shape a life full of discipline and meaning. I respect this self-chosen, hard-won goodness more than I respect the namby-pambies who have never had a fright when they looked into the mirror and saw where their lives were leading them. Have they ever really looked at their natures, or do they just docilely accept authority's word for what their natures are? For natures are as varied as individual fingerprints, and what may be good for*

my roommate might be shirking the real challenges for me. Or vice versa, of course. Besides, if goodness only means 'innocence,' if it only means never experimenting, never straying from the accepted paths, then the whole concept of redemption—on which Christianity is founded—becomes meaningless."

"You have plunged into deep waters here," Miss Petrie wrote under my "A minus," "and I admire your courage. I, too, have worried over the 'different kinds' of goodness and concluded, as you seem to be in the process of doing, that there is no formula for the way I know I must live—which sometimes makes it very hard. The 'minus' is because of all the split infinitives. You really have to watch those."

It was January and my father and Fiona Petrie still had not met. There had not even been an opportunity for me to prepare the ground. Shortly before Christmas vacation, it had been discovered that my wisdom teeth were impacted, and, since I was still covered under my step-father's hospitalization insurance, it was decided that I would go to visit my mother for Christmas and have a dental surgeon remove all four teeth under anesthetic at the hospital. "I'll miss you, of course," said my father, when I phoned him to tell him the news, "but God knows I can't compete with a paid-up Blue Cross policy." He had chuckled softly over the phone, and I suspected he was secretly relieved to have a little breather from me after the Thanksgiving scene.

I did not tell my mother about it, partly because I didn't want her to fear for my safety around a father who drank, but mainly because the scene—and the drinking—might be fairly attributed to my own sneaky behavior. I had let my father think I was innocent and "unspoiled" when I wasn't. But, as I lay in the hospital bed for a day and a night, I went over and over what had happened, and had to admit to myself that if I had had it to do over—starting from the moment I had been reunited with my father—I would have done nothing differently: except destroy those letters. Did that make me a liar and a hypocrite? I supposed so. But what had been done had been done. If my father had been so set on keeping his prize horse safe in the barn, then maybe he should have stayed around all those years and looked after it. Besides, what business was anybody's private love life to anybody else? I hadn't questioned him about what he and Myrna did until five AM up in "W. O.'s" garage apartment.

Of course, things were different for men. But why were they different? Why were fillies cautioned to stay in the barn and stallions encouraged to romp about the fields, sowing wild oats? Why had I been so careful to pretend I was still in the barn, when I had been outside to have a look around? The more I thought over my motives for playing the innocent ingénue, the more I realized they probably boiled down to a single thing: my market value. Was Lovegood College, then, behind all its traditions and candlelit ceremonies and quaint, maidenly rules, simply a very successful market for brides? Judging from the number of engaged sophomores—judging from the hallowed place we'd made for ourselves in the college-boy jingles—it certainly seemed possible.

My father had asked, in his coup de grâce, why I said I was happy at that school. *Was* I happy? Most of the time I was. There were small irritations—such as the night Hermione Broadstead had cried because I was reading with a flashlight under my covers after lights-out. I was torturing her, she said, because she had to decide whether or not it was her duty, under the honor code, to report me. Hermione was nineteen years old. Shouldn't people of nineteen have more serious ethical problems on their mind? But I had turned off my flashlight because I was fond of Hermione with her old-fashioned dependability and her generosity (she was always slipping "surprises" under her roommates' pillows) and even the ubiquitous little heart-shaped lavender sachets she scattered all over our closets and drawers. In a way, she was like Lovegood: she stood for a safety and a simplicity that I hadn't quite had enough of yet.

Several weeks into the spring semester, I came out of classes one morning to find a telephone message in my mailbox: my father had phoned saying he would be driving up that afternoon and hoped he could see me and take me out to dinner. He would arrive sometime between four thirty and five.

I took this to be a sign of reconciliation. We had not seen each other since the Thanksgiving weekend, although we had exchanged several cheerful and newsy letters—carefully avoiding any reference to "the evening." Now he was exercising perfect tact, I thought, by coming up for the afternoon like this, rather than suggesting I come home with him for another weekend. This way, we could feel each other out, quietly looking into each other's eyes over a table in a restaurant, assessing how we stood with each other before we started over. I must wear just the right dress.

As I came out of the mailroom, I saw Miss Petrie floating ahead of me in her swinging skirt and high heels. What was I waiting for? Wouldn't this afternoon, when my father and I were beginning again, also be an ideal time to instigate another beginning?

"Miss Petrie!"

She stopped and waited for me. By now, a definite bond of affection had been established between us, and she always gave me a pleased and rather possessive smile when I sought her out.

I told her my father was coming to the school late that afternoon and if she was still around it would mean a lot for me to have him meet her. She said she'd be delighted, and would wait for us in the upstairs parlor, where she would be waiting for Miss Olafson anyway, since this was one of those days the gym teacher stayed late to give private tennis lessons on our new indoor court.

A little after four fifteen, I put on my beige lamb's wool polo coat and climbed the stairs to the fourth floor. It had come into my romantic imagination that I would stand out on the top balcony, between the two central columns, and watch for my father's car as it came down the hilly street on which we had first approached this school together. I remembered how he had looked admiringly up at the imposing facade and said, "Now that must have been some place to live." I had a superstitious wish for him to look up and see me standing there all alone in the coat he had bought for me, a devoted daughter looking small and protected between the mammoth white columns of the old plantation home.

Many cars came down the hill, but no black-and-white Mercury Montclair. My hands grew cold in the raw air, and the colors of the cars became harder to make out as the early winter dusk closed in.

A car came into the college grounds, but it was an old green Studebaker, and I resumed my fruitless scan of the distant cars descending the hill. The car door of the Studebaker slammed, and the *crunch, crunch* of a man's footsteps approached below on the gravel. I looked down and recognized my father's loose, rolling walk. Everything looked darker about him, and then I realized it was because he was wearing a dark overcoat and I had grown used to him in light summer suits. I started to call out to him, but he looked so absorbed in his thoughts; I was afraid it might startle, or even anger, him if I were suddenly to shout "hey!" or "yoo-hoo!" Besides, the whole point was for him to have seen me first. But why was he driving that undistinguished old Studebaker?

I rushed down the four flights of stairs and found him chatting politely with the girl on reception duty. "Oh, good girl," he said, when he saw me in my coat, "you're all ready to go." He seemed happy to see me, but his face fell a little when I told him I wanted him to step upstairs for just a few minutes and meet Miss Petrie. "She's my favorite teacher," I said, "and I admire her more than just about any woman I know."

"Well," he said, squaring his shoulders and making the best of it, "by all means, let me meet this paragon. It's just that I promised to be back at a sensible hour tonight, and I want us to have a nice long dinner."

"It won't take very long," I assured him. But my hopes fell a little. Maybe I should have waited and introduced them at a later time. But wasn't time, more than ever, of the essence when he was already "promising" somebody to be home at a sensible hour?

Miss Petrie was sitting in one corner of the sofa, grading papers on her lap. The upstairs parlor, with its flowered chintzes and soft lamps and hunting prints, was a cozy, congenial room, and the English teacher, with her dainty gold-framed reading glasses, looked as relaxed as if she were bent over her work in her own home.

When I introduced my father to her, she cordially extended her right hand to him, at the same time giving a little push to the glasses, which fell gracefully to her bosom and hung upside down from the grosgrain ribbons to which they were fastened.

"I've heard so much about you," she said, in her solemn cello-voice, "and need I tell you it was all glowing? Please sit down."

"Well, my daughter seems to admire you pretty glowingly, too," he said. He sat down in a wing chair perpendicular to the sofa, on the other side of Miss Petrie's lamp. I sat down beside Miss Petrie on the sofa.

They were both well-brought-up people who knew how to fill up silence with formal compliments and pleasantries. She told him I resembled him remarkably and he told her it was kind of her to say so—for his sake. She told him it was a pleasure for her to have me in her class. "I oughtn't to say this in front of her, but I look forward to her papers just to see what she's going to say next. Her mind works in such interesting ways."

"I would like to see some of those papers," said my father, and then we both looked away from each other. Remembering, no doubt, that he had already seen some other "papers" that involved me.

There followed a silence that must be filled up.

"Did you—," Miss Petrie began, addressing my father.

"Are you—," he began at the same time.

Then they both laughed uneasily. "You first," he said.

"No, I insist. *You* first."

"I was only going to ask if you were by any chance one of the Beaufort Petries."

"I am indeed." She sounded pleased. "I am one of the few still left. Too many girls ran in the family. At least," and she smiled ruefully, "I've held on to the name."

"Yes!" replied my father animatedly. Then he seemed to feel he had been too animated. He sank back into the wing chair, looking pensive.

There was a very long silence in which we all sat looking very interested in what anybody might say next.

Then in bounded Miss Olafson in her coat and tennis shoes, her tennis racket in its case under her arm.

"Well, well," she said, grinning, "I'm so glad I'm not too late to meet the glorious father." My father, who was on his feet at once, offered his hand to her hearty grip.

Then they talked tennis for a few minutes, Miss Petrie looking from one to the other with interest and relief. We were all on our feet by then.

"That wasn't so bad," said my father, as we headed toward the parking lot. "They're both nice women. The Petries are a very distinguished family. I often heard my mother speak of them. *She* seems a sad person, though. Now that Olafson is a cheerful old girl."

"What happened to your demonstrator?" I asked, as he opened the creaking door on the passenger side of the Studebaker and waved me in with a mock bow.

"Ah, it was never 'my' demonstrator. It was W. O.'s demonstrator. We sold it to a man in town who said he admired the way I looked in it and maybe some of the look would rub off on him. Now W. O. says I have to look good in this for awhile, until we can get it off the used car lot. Hop in. With our combined beauty, we ought to be able to transform it into a desirable chariot in no time."

Over dinner, he went on in this mocking, high-flown manner, and I couldn't decide whether he was in arrogantly high spirits or desperately low spirits, which he camouflaged with this lordly, sarcastic banter.

Over dessert he told me had some bad news and some good news. Which would I prefer to hear first?

"The bad," I said. "Then there will be something to look forward to."

"Well, I *hope* there will," he replied in the gentlest tone he had used all evening.

The bad news was that he had "overextended himself" this year, and, since the car business was terrible at the moment, I was going to have to contribute . . . I was going to have to contribute quite a bit . . . if I wanted to stay at that happy college.

The good news was that he and Myrna had been married last weekend.

. . .

That summer I earned money as a lifeguard at a
girls' camp. During my sophomore year at
Lovegood, I was the recipient of financial aid
kindly found for me through the president, that
same agreeable figure who had served us lemonade on a hot July day and invited my father to
remove his jacket. For part of the money I was
obliged to work in the library, shelving books
and making bulletin board displays, which I enjoyed a lot. The other part of the money came
from one of the college's many endowment
scholarships. All I had to do for that part was to
write a thank-you letter to the man who had established the scholarship in honor of his mother,
who had been a Lovegood girl.

During my sophomore year at Lovegood, I
visited my father, but not as frequently as the
previous year. He and Myrna put up a cheerful
married front, but he often wore the sheepish
look I had seen that night in the diner after our

scene, and, as for Myrna, she became graver and more dignified and hardly ever giggled anymore.

I slept at my aunt's house when I visited them, and after we had all had supper and sat around and talked, and my father and Myrna got in their Studebaker—which W. O. had decided to give to my father (as a reward for marrying his sister-in-law?)—I would get undressed and go to bed and my aunt would come in and sit in a rocking chair with her knitting and literally talk me to sleep. She made fun of herself for being a lonely old woman crazy for company, but, all the same, she would tell me, there were lots of old stories she could tell about my father, stories I might be glad I had heard someday, even if I had yawned through the telling. One story she told me was about when they were all children: she and the judge and the brother who had died during an operation and my father. Everybody was in the kitchen one evening, helping their mother dry the supper dishes, everybody but my father, that was. *He,* the youngest, the precious last-born, was standing outside, his back to the house, watching the sunset in a dreamy, faraway manner. "Make him come in and help," demanded my aunt, but their mother had said, "Let him be, let him be. He is such a different child, my baby, and one day, you wait and see, he will be a great man."

My aunt told me that my father was by nature a perfectionist and it made him hard on people. "But the person in all the world he's hardest on is himself," she said.

My aunt also told me that it had been a good thing that Myrna had a little income of her own. "I don't know what they would have done without it," said my aunt. "Your father really overextended himself last year, but he wanted you to be a carefree college girl. I told him you were perfectly able to help out, and so you are."

I graduated with a 4.0 average from Lovegood College and threw my roses into the fountain. I never did get into the Lovegood Christian Association. Because of my excellent grades I was able to get a full scholarship to Chapel Hill (where the rules were less stringent, and the ratio of men to women was ten to one; the reason why, in those days, women were not allowed to enter the university until they were juniors: the temptation of all those boys would be devastating, the authorities felt).

I remained friends with Miss Petrie, and got to like Miss Olafson a lot, too. They sometimes invited me, during my second year at Lovegood, to go home with them for supper. Then Miss Olafson would drive me back to school. They had a warm, comfortable apartment, and Miss Olafson did all the cooking, as she said Miss Petrie's lack of coordination also extended to kitchen matters. She teased Miss Petrie about it. The first time they showed me the upstairs of their apartment, I didn't know what to say when Miss Olafson pointed out their bedroom. There was just one double bed. But then Miss Olafson explained they used the other bedroom for Miss

There was just one double bed

Petrie's library and study. "Fiona stays up late grading papers," the gym teacher said with her friendly grin. "Me, thank God, I leave my work at school."

A few years later, I met my old history teacher Miss McCorkle on a bus, and she told me she was now Mrs. Snyder. She had met her husband, a widower, in the adult Sunday school class at the Presbyterian church to which we all used to march, wearing our white gloves and our pillbox hats with their little wisps of veil. We got to talking about old Lovegood girls, who had gone on to what college and married whom, and then she told me that Miss Olafson and Miss Petrie had gone. "Carol Olafson got an offer from a college—one of those offers you just can't refuse—and Fiona stayed on at Lovegood for another year," said Mrs. Snyder, née McCorkle, "but she pined her heart out all year, and now she's gone to join her, even though there was no teaching job for her in that town."

I sat there beside my old history teacher thinking: so it probably wouldn't have worked out with my father anyway.

"And how is your father?" asked Mrs. Snyder, thinking she was getting us onto a more cheerful subject.

I had to tell her he had died during my junior year.

"Good heavens! That fine figure of a man? What was it—heart attack?"

I told her no, actually it had been "by his own choice." That was the phrase I used in those days. I explained to her that it had been coming for a long time, that he had been a perfectionist and life had disappointed him, but most of all he had disappointed himself. On top of that, business got very bad, and there was a serious drinking problem. His second wife had tried to save him, but he hadn't wanted to be saved.

"Well, I'm sorry to hear this," said the history teacher. She looked sternly out the window of the bus. "But I will certainly pray for him," she said, after a minute. "And Mr. Snyder will, too."

. . .

In the recent Lovegood Alumnae Bulletin in which I saw that Mrs. Elizabeth McCorkle Snyder has given a memorial donation "in memory of Miss Carol Olafson, former P.E. and Health teacher," I also noted that the college had reached its $5.4 million capital fund-raising drive a year early. My donation is included among those dollars. I have given money faithfully over the years to that college, adding to the amount each time my own fortunes increased. How I would explain my loyalty to Lovegood to somebody like that stylish, cynical woman on the airplane, I don't know. I probably couldn't give a cynical listener any satisfactory answer.

But I tell myself it is for a variety of reasons, some idealistic, some sentimental.

Like that old Lovegood family daughter in the school pageant who, in her quaking voice, tells Dr. Manley Phipps, enlightened Presbyterian educator, I, too, could say: "I hope that future generations of Lovegood girls will be as happy and carefree as I was in that house." Or words to that effect.

I also like the idea of some girl like myself—her heart divided between the traditions and glories of the past and the uncertain demands of the future—leaning her cheek against one of those magnificent white columns and knowing she may dream and study and play the innocent ingénue a little longer.

But perhaps most of all I cherish the image of some father—beset by the bitter intelligence of how soon youth is over, how sour some dreams may turn—who nevertheless can lay his head down on his pillow and rest secure in the knowledge that his daughter rests and dreams in a protected and honorable place, gathering her young strengths for the coming fray.

Waltzing with the Black Crayon

Paul Engle should get a posthumous medal from the coast guard for all the lives he saved.

—KURT VONNEGUT AT THE MEMORIAL SERVICE FOR
THE FOUNDER OF THE IOWA WRITERS' WORKSHOP

My side of this story begins in London in the summer of 1966, when my English husband of less than one year was running an experiment on me in our Chelsea garden. We were sitting in the shade of a mulberry tree so ancient that its branches had to be propped up with stakes. Hoping to root out the source of my unhappiness, Ian was asking me the same question over and over again.

Ian was a medical doctor who had switched to psychotherapy. An independent sort, he took inspiration from unorthodox sources. The present inquisition, which I was willingly under-going, was one he had borrowed from Scien-tology. The auditor asked the client the same question until he or she answered the truth. For this process the Scientologists used something called an E-Meter, a poor cousin to the lie detector, devised from two seven-ounce V8 juice cans stripped of their labels and wired to a galvanometer. When the client clutching the cans finally spoke the truth, the needle on the meter stopped jerking around and floated freely. The client was supposed to feel a floating sense of relief as well.

We weren't using the apparatus. Ian said he could read me as accurately as any V8 juice cans could. He kept asking the agreed-upon ques-tion, pushing the truth to the surface. It was like having a well-intentioned person firmly squeez-ing a pimple.

Then suddenly I answered truly, the pimple burst, I felt a surge of release, and we agreed that the experiment had been a success. It had indeed. Within the month I had left England. Three months later I was living in a shabby-genteel hotel on Manhattan's East Side, walking to work every morning to my fact-checking job at *The Saturday Evening Post.* In between phone calls to the Farmers Federation ("I'm in the research department at *The Saturday Evening Post;* can you tell me whether a cow has four or six udders?") or the U.S. Air Force ("Colonel, is it true that the Delta Dagger can be off the ground in three seconds?"), I typed furtively on a lengthening story about a newly married couple's wretched vacation in Majorca with the doctor-husband's disturbed child. In the *Post's* morgue, I read a back-issue feature on the Iowa Writers' Workshop, where people like Flannery O'Connor had flowered into their potential. At night I lay in my bumpy bed at the Pickwick Arms and read library books chosen to keep up my courage (*Invisible Man,* all of Henry Miller, and a caustically funny fabulist of the current state of planet Earth named Kurt Vonnegut, Jr.). I was intrigued by the "Junior" and wondered what the father was like; I also wondered about the woman I shared a bathroom with. She wept a lot and her bowels were all to pieces. I never did see her. I came to think of her as a doppelgänger who had sense enough to be appalled and terrified by what I had done.

"Why can't you be a writer?" my husband had asked, about forty times in a row, under the mulberry tree in our garden in Chelsea.

"Because I'm afraid I might fail," I admitted at last. And forthwith left him, and stepped off into empty space.

My life during that Manhattan autumn wore all the outward signs of foolishness and failure. I was twenty-nine years old, with a second defaulted marriage behind me, not one penny in the bank, and a single completed short story

Christina's earliest typewriter

about an English vicar who sees God, writes a book, and goes on an American book tour (this was for a writing assignment at the London City Literary Institute, where I had met my second husband). And not even a bathroom to myself.

Yet from below the grid of this quotidian reality on which I marched back and forth between Pickwick Arms and *Saturday Evening Post,* I felt frequent bracing updrafts from an ulterior psychic stream pulsing stubbornly along toward its own destination. My old energy had returned, that elated focus I had experienced in my early twenties when I had boarded a freighter for Europe because that's where I presumed Americans had to go in order to turn into writers.

Surprises happened daily in New York. Many bore the quality of augury or plot. Even when they were awful, they took on the heightened significance of character-building episodes in a narrative. My passport along with my wallet was stolen from my office at the *Post*. I reported the theft to the police but did nothing about getting a new passport. A kindly civilized man took me out to a fine dinner, then gave me a tour of his office and suddenly threw himself on me. I could have pushed him aside, or simply run for the elevator, but instead heard an aria of crisp, vile epithets issue eloquently from my mouth. He looked aghast and fled from *me*.

An uncle in Alabama died and left me five thousand dollars, meant to be a friendly slap because I had neglected him (my cousin got two digits more than I). Then a friend met in Europe wrote me out of the blue, announcing that she was now in Iowa City, enrolled in the Writers' Workshop: why didn't I come out, too? I quit my job, checked out of the Pickwick Arms, and boarded an airplane that flew right into the middle of an Iowa snowstorm and dropped me into more white empty space than I had ever seen in my life. Naturally, the airline had lost all my luggage.

Iowa was one of the most exciting influences
of my life. And it was an accident,
like everything else in the sixties.

—KURT VONNEGUT REMINISCING ON
11 DECEMBER 1997 AT HIS HOME ON
EAST 48TH STREET IN MANHATTAN

"You ask what I would have done if I hadn't gone to Iowa," mused Vonnegut. "Died of boredom, I guess. I was *elated* when George Starbuck called me from Iowa in August 1965. Robert Lowell had backed out at the last minute, and they needed another teacher in the workshop. Paul Engle didn't know my work, most people thought I was a science-fiction writer, but George was my friend. And the job came with a salary. For that I would have joined the paratroopers. Up until then I had been stuck in a house on Cape Cod with six kids. Iowa in contrast was a party. Everybody in the workshop was so interesting. There was a war on, and we had draft dodgers, and, no offense meant, we even had women who'd been married and divorced. By the way, what ever happened to that disturbed little boy in your first novel?"

"You mean the real person?" I said.

"Sure, the real person."

"Oh, he grew up and went to Oxford, and . . ."

Kurt started to laugh.

"Wait a minute, I'm not finished. He got a double first in math and philosophy."

"Then he didn't have a screw loose, after all."

"No, I think he was just mad as hell."

"The only surprise was," Kurt went on, "when I got out to Iowa, I learned I was also expected to teach a course in fiction. I had majored in chemistry at Cornell and anthropology at the University of Chicago. Well, I decided I was supposed to teach technique, so I picked some books and then the class and I set out to discover together how the trick was done. We did *Dubliners, Treasure Island, Invisible Man,* and, let's see, *Madame Bovary,* and *Alice in Wonderland,* and some Chekhov stories.

"The first thing I told my students about writing was: you've got to take care of your reader. The average age of you guys was about twenty-eight. You'd been developed socially and you knew how to dance. All I tried to do was impress upon you that you had to be a good date as a writer. You had to be reader-friendly. The last story in *Dubliners,* 'The Dead,' is *not* reader-friendly. In the first two pages, you've met nine people. *You must not do this!*

"And you've got to give your reader familiar props along the way. In *Alice in Wonderland,* remember, when she's falling down the hole there are all these familiar, comforting objects along the sides: cupboards and bookshelves and maps. Orange marmalade. . . .

"Another thing we discovered about technique: If you want to write a book about politics, don't introduce a love element, or it will take over the story and the story *ends* when the couple gets together. If your purpose is something else—as it was for Ralph Ellison—you're better off without the love element. And he was.

"Another rule I tried to impress upon you: *MAKE YOUR CHARACTER WANT SOMETHING.* There was a nun in one of my workshop sections who wrote a wonderful story about this nun who goes through an entire day with a piece of dental floss stuck in her teeth. [Laughter] All you guys were reaching around in your mouths while we were discussing that story. The character in that story *wanted* something!

"Then there was this Hungarian student. I think he was there the year before you arrived. He had gotten out during the revolution and come over here and gone to an American university. He kept turning in these tepid stories about love affairs in American dormitories. I finally told him in a conference, 'Look, these are too tame. Try something a little more dramatic.' He went away and came back with a story that was pure dynamite, about this Hungarian nobleman in World War II who goes around in his van rescuing the wounded from the battlefields. Well, he's just rescued a soldier who's had both legs blown off and he's carrying him back to the van when the Germans come over the hill in retreat. They take his van and supplies and leave him there in the middle of nowhere with a double amputee in his arms. It was an absolutely *riveting* story. The trouble was, it was written by someone else. After that, he vanished from the workshop.

"Of course I had students who refused to take my advice. Remember Ronnie ————? She turned in a story whose first sentence was, 'Listen, you dumb motherfuckers.' I said, 'Listen, Ronnie, you just can't *do* that.' But she did.

"Once the Iowa legislature tried to close us down because a student—not Ronnie—had used *fuck* in a story. But they couldn't touch us. We had private money supporting the workshop. The citizens of Iowa weren't paying anything for us. That was Paul Engle's doing. He was a hell of a good money-raiser. His father had been a horse trader, and when Paul was a boy he was the one who stuck the ginger up the horses' behinds just before they were shown."

I write with a big black crayon, you know, grasped in a grubby, kindergarten fist. You're more of an impressionist. If you want to kind of try what I do, take life seriously but none of the people in it. The people are fools and I say so the instant they're onstage. I don't let them prove it slowly.

—LETTER FROM KURT VONNEGUT, WEST BARNSTABLE, MASSACHUSETTS, TO GAIL GODWIN, STILL IN IOWA CITY, 25 NOVEMBER 1967

When I arrived in January 1967 in the snow-storm, Kurt Vonnegut was beginning the last semester of his second and final teaching year in the workshop. He already had one foot out the door. He had won a Guggenheim and would soon be on his way to Germany to refresh his memory for his novel in progress about being an American prisoner of war during the fire-bombing of Dresden, *Slaughterhouse-Five.* I had wanted the creator of Eliot Rosewater and none other to read my (now novella-length) story

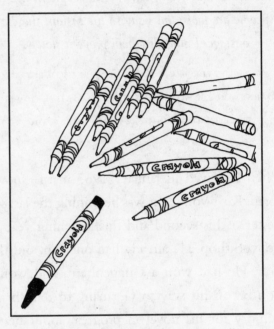

"I write with a big black crayon . . ."

about the wretched couple and the disturbed little boy driving one another crazy in Majorca, but there was a brief bout of despair: Vonnegut had become so in demand that his workshop section was overflowing. Sorry, but you'll have to choose someone else.

Then, at the last minute, Vonnegut generously agreed to take on an extra section because I was not the only one in despair.

The sections met once a week, and we critiqued one another's mimeographed work. Jane Barnes, whose forte was social satire, turned in a devilishly funny story called "Coming of Age in Washington, D.C." She wore big swooping hats to the English building and was engaged to another Vonnegut student, John Casey. She had an enviable collection of rejection letters from none other than Roger Angell at *The New Yorker*. Inspired by her example, I was soon amassing a similar collection of letters from Angell myself. ("Dear Miss Godwin, I am sorry to disappoint you again, but you are getting better and better.") Several years later, Jane, who was by then married to John Casey, published an impressive fictional autobiography of Lenin's wife, *I, Krupskaya.*

In the spring of 1967, John Casey was another stimulant to my ambition. He had a novel *under option* by a major publisher. He would sometimes read his friends enticing little snatches from this work in progress, sophisticated exchanges between East Coast college kids. I don't know what became of that book, but he later published a dream of a novel set in Iowa, *An American Romance,* and went on to win the 1989 National Book Award for his novel *Spartina,* whose world is a far cry from the college venue of witty smoothies.

Another Vonnegut student was John Irving, already married and with a small son. At Irving's twenty-fifth birthday party, he played his guests a tape of the music for the film score of his first novel, *Setting Free the Bears.* He hadn't finished the novel, no publisher or film person had laid eyes on it, but John had chosen the music he wanted. ("It was from Carl Orff's

Carmina Burana," John Irving recalled thirty years later. "I often did that, picked the music for the film before I finished the book. Call it my mayhem confidence.")

"I knew John Irving would make it big," said Kurt as we reminisced. "He was always just so preposterously *funny*! And John Casey, you know, we gave him that American Academy grant for a three-year stipend, and the three years are up and he's just turned in an eleven-hundred-page novel. I have this little device on my telephone that measures the state of people's happiness, and John sounded really *up*. And you, you've become a big shot."

"I don't feel like a big shot. Writing gets harder and harder."

"It's supposed to," Kurt said.

("Can you remember what it was like, working on *Setting Free the Bears* with Kurt at the work-shop?" I asked John Irving.

"Oh, for instance, he told me that I was interested in a certain young woman's underwear to an excess of what my readers would be," said John.

"And did you take his advice?"

"Not to the degree that I probably should have," Irving wryly admitted. "But he also said I wrote with so much enthusiasm. He told me, 'Never lose that enthusiasm. So many writers are *unenthusiastic* about their work.' ")

The forty-five-year-old Vonnegut of my own conferences, his gangly length tilted back in a swivel chair, desert boots on the metal desk, cigarette and ashtray never out of sight, looked much as he does now, except for the white mustache and give or take a few extra rumples in the face. In those one-to-one sessions, he was as loose and playful as a Zen master. He had read my novella-length story, later to become *The Perfectionists,* about the ill-matched couple and the disturbed little boy driving one another berserk on a Spanish island, and had written comments in light pencil in the margins: "Lovely." "First-rate." Or "No: sandbagging flashback!"

"I'm thinking of expanding it into a novel," I said during a conference. "What do you think?"

"Oh, I think it's just great as it is," Vonnegut said.

In our next conference I told him I had decided to go ahead and turn it into a novel anyway.

"Great idea," he exclaimed enthusiastically.

"You were different," I told Kurt Vonnegut in December 1997, the end of the twentieth century in our faces, a whole new millennium about to roll over. I had just delivered my tenth novel to my publisher. He was winding down his book tour for *Timequake,* a narrative summary, with autobiographical digressions, about an unfinished novel that he got tired of writing, in which we were forced to relive an entire decade all over again, making the same mistakes. Vonnegut had announced that *Timequake* would be his final novel.

"All my books are in print, and I have nothing else to say. There are lots of talented young artists out there, let them have their chance."

I protested.

"Oh, well," he conceded, with a strange smile. "If you must know, I have one more novel in me. You want to hear it? It's about my affair with O. J. Simpson. I met him in a locker room once in Buffalo and asked him to sign my football, not realizing that this was a code for propositioning someone. . . ."

I had fallen for it, as other protesters before me surely had done.

"I think of you as a prophet like Jonah," I told Vonnegut. "You say woe to the planet and draw dire scenarios, and people see their awful, ridiculous selves, and so God relents and decides to keep things going a little longer."

(John Irving tells me there's a current bumper

sticker with the globe on a spit, roasting over a fire, and a Vonnegut quotation underneath: "WE COULD HAVE SAVED IT BUT WE WERE TOO DARN CHEAP AND LAZY.")

"Well, the whale has certainly spit me up in some odd places," Kurt acknowledged.

"When we were your students, you let us work it out for ourselves," I told him. "Yet your being there for us did the trick. After you left Iowa, the teachers I had were—they had their own agendas."

(One of them explained to me that he couldn't read my 250-page manuscript of *The Perfectionists* until duck-hunting season was over. After he read it, on a flight to California, he had to admit that he was lukewarm. I tried to pin him down to specifics, but he was vague. "Do you think I'll ever make it?" I finally demanded at the end of our conference. "Gee, Gail. How old are you?" "Thirty," I said. He squinted at his watch as though consulting an oracle. "Well, I don't know," he said, "I published my first novel at twenty-four."

My teacher after him was a dynamic little magician who played writing games with us in class. ["Today, we're going to be an Irish monk in the seventh century who has just unearthed an ancient manuscript that turns out to be written by . . . SCHEHERAZADE! Are you ready?"]

I loved his classes for their sheer excitement, but on 11 December 1968, the day after my new agent, John Hawkins, sold the third draft of *The Perfectionists* to David Segal at Harper and Row, my little magician told me in a private conference that he was happy for me but also sad. He had been urging me toward more experimental sleights of hand, and warned me that if I persisted in this dogged attention to reality I might end up like . . . well, someone like John Updike.)

"All I did in those private conferences with you guys," recalled Kurt, thirty years later, "was to say, '*Trust me.* What I'm going to do now is open your mouth, very gently, with these two fingers, and then I'm going to reach in—being very careful not to bruise your epiglottis—and catch hold of this little tape inside you and slowly, very carefully and gently, pull it out of you. It's your tape, and it's the only tape like that in the world."

(When I quoted Vonnegut's "tape" theory to John Irving and asked John if he would care to sum up the essence of the tape that had come out of Kurt Vonnegut's mouth, he thought a minute and then said: "Irreverence for human beings and institutions. Kindness for individuals.")

Kurt Vonnegut in New York City to Gail Godwin in Woodstock, New York, 14 September 1979

"Dearest Gail—

I thank you for your kind remarks about *Jailbird.* We try to run a class operation here, but fail more often than not. The luckiest thing I ever did was to teach at Iowa for

Christina's ultimate typewriter

those two years. I picked up a very classy extended family that way. It made you and John and John and some others quality relatives of mine for life. I used to be in this trade all alone. Suddenly I was a member of a really great gang. I never tire of asking you and the rest, 'How goes it?' If you are ever in trouble, I will take you in."

Mother and Daughter Ghosts, A Memoir

⬥⬥⬥

I have wanted to write something about this for ten years. Now a request comes and I accept it as a summons. At first I thought: I would use the fictional form of one of my Christina stories, which were inaugurated this past summer, also in response to a request ("We are putting together an issue on the theme of writers' childhood experiences of religion, and if you had something in your files that might . . ."). I didn't have anything in my files, so I wrote my first Christina story, in which Christina, age eleven, first avails herself of the sacrament of Penance. Then a few weeks later came another invitation, this time for something set in the South, and I wrote my second Christina story, in which Christina, age fifteen, goes to visit rich relatives in Texas and is tempted/repelled by their largess. I began to envision a whole collection of Christina stories to carry me through the rest of my life. Before consciousness fades, I hope to have chronicled Christina becoming eligible for Medicare (if it still exists!), Christina's ninetieth birthday party, Christina's final codicil, and so forth.

But since this story belongs equally to two people, was indeed chronicled by two people, my mother and me, in our separate journals—and for another reason that I hope will make itself abundantly clear in the final paragraphs—I have decided to cast it in the memoir form.

In July of 1989, K. and I went on one of those psychology-and-spirituality journeys at Kanuga, the Episcopal Conference Center in Hendersonville. I had read about it in a brochure and it sounded interesting, so I invited her, flew down to Asheville, and off we went to explore ourselves together. It was a slightly different take on the mother-daughter outings to which we treated ourselves every few years, the last one having been a weeklong retreat with the Sisters of All Saints in Catonsville, Maryland. The All Saints week had been an idyll, perhaps because silence and chant and communal prayer and the example of some really good women had been part of the package, but this time we had chosen to immerse ourselves in a less orthodox, talkier brew and ended up swimming with my demons, her demons, and probably, by association, the demons of some others we may have gotten confused with our own.

Even before the first session of our journeys got under way, my mother and I had started to misbehave. When I was a little girl, or as K. used to say, "when you and I were growing up," we had played a wicked little game in which we took turns imitating people or drawing cartoons of them and then guessing the identities. Nobody

was sacred and nobody was exempt, except ourselves, of course. Eventually, we abandoned the
full-scale acting and the drawing and played the
game with raised eyebrows, rolling eyeballs,
codes, weird smiles, and innuendos. K. was a
master of the devastating "innocent" understate-
ment. She was particularly hard on the humor-
less, the sanctimonious, the intrusively personal,
and anything too breathlessly New Age. And
here we were with at least a hundred new people
to play the game on, and I'm afraid we started to
do it immediately.

But then, in the first evenings session, K., I
thought, turned on me. She refused to do the
exercise assigned by the conference leaders. We
were each given a pad of paper and a set of
Crayolas and told to make a picture of—I forget
exactly what: our expectations for the week, our
idea of a spiritual entrance space to the week,
something like that. Then those who wanted to
share could pin their artwork on the wall. I immediately started planning something impressive
to draw, then looked over at K. to see if she'd al-

ready started. She was in the act of putting her crayons and paper beneath her seat.

When she straightened up, a weird little smile on her face, she said, "I prefer to *think* my spiritual space."

"Well, I'm going to do mine," I said. I felt put down. For revenge, I did a cartoon of her, all in blue, as she was, hunched up in her superiority bubble. I made it look like an egg, she wasn't even hatched yet! I pinned it up on the wall with the rainbows and hearts and sunshines of others' expectations for the week. It was recognizably she. She made no comment as it stayed pinned up on the communal wall, day after day.

We shared a room in the main building, the inn. Our closest times that week were at night, after the journaling classes and art therapy and lectures on personality types and spirituality by ministers and therapists. We lay side by side in our single beds and discussed the people, those we liked, those we were curious about, those we had reservations about (I was put off by his lecture. Lack of reverence for God, and a little too much reverence for himself—plus *what,* pray tell, is a "user-friendly church"?), and those who would have been parody fodder in the old days (the man who came on to K. at the evening fellowship hour with an uninvited hug and, "We're all here, you know, because we're not all here— ha, ha"). We'd both taken the Myers–Briggs (another mother-daughter team) for an extra ten dollars each, and speculated on our single difference: her INFJ to my INTJ. How it had affected our fifty-year-long relationship, my being an introverted intuitive *thinking* judging daughter and her being an introverted intuitive *feeling* judging mother? We talked about some of the past, the recent past when she divorced her second husband after thirty-eight years of marriage and went to live by herself for the first time in her life, and the far distant past when she was a young mother living with her mother and me, those years when it was just us, "growing up together."

Then, in our shared room in the inn, we would write in our respective journals. I was al-

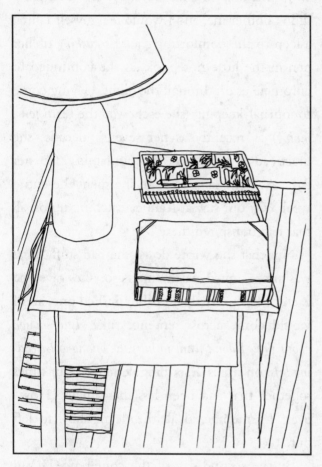

We would write in our respective journals

ways the first to shut up shop, her bed lamp didn't bother me, and I would feel myself falling asleep to the comforting *scratch-scratching* of her pen in the little notebook, as she continued to chronicle us on through the night. Having come to journal-keeping (she eschewed the term *journaling*) as recently as her seventh decade, she practiced a scrupulous accountability for her days. As I was later to read, she spent the entire week *after* our stay at Kanuga catching up on all that had transpired there.

Not that she wrote down the bad stuff. That was more my department. Also, she gave me each of her journals after she finished one, and I would come across sentences like, *But enough about that, I don't want to hurt the one who is reading this,* on pages describing certain of our times together that had been less than idyllic. However, *I* remembered all the detail she had left out.

By the second day of the conference, I had begun to act the part of the sullen sidekick daughter. It was the oddest thing. I knew I was acting. It wasn't a part I wanted to play or ever *had* played before, but I found I was sewn into my costume. And the more unattractive and resentful I became, the more K. shone. She flirted with the popular lecturer, telling him her younger son was also a handsome, magnetic teacher. She sat in a rocking chair on the porch, embroidering a kneeler for her dead elder son, and listened to the sad stories of others. She said sharp, witty things at mealtimes, and on the last afternoon made a woman in her grief work-shop a knotted necklace out of blue and yellow yarns because the woman said she needed to take away something of K.'s as a talisman.

The two low points in my week coincided with two triumphs in hers. The first was a group session in active imagination, in which our leader told us to descend via elevator into the throne room of our psyche and have an audience with the king and queen. We closed our eyes and he led us, hypnotist-style, through the steps of the descent, from which we were to return with our own encounters. Even though I chose a thick rope for my Ariadne's thread, I had a bad trip. Afterward, many people (including me) raised their hands to tell about their experience. I was not called on, but cornered the leader on a path afterward. He said I might need to do some work on my inner Lover and next time I tried active imagination to take along a knight or a warrior. K., of course, did not raise her hand and share with others, but in our room that night she read aloud to me a description of her trip from her journal:

K.'s "trip" in creative imagination. Didn't bother with Ariadne's thread. I wasn't afraid. Nor did I show proper deference to anyone, even king or queen. Down the elevator to center—a crucifix was in front of me as I got off—shining gold, elaborate—was it barring the way or answering my "Put on the whole armor of the Lord"? Another at [sic] to door throne room. Big robot opened it. Medieval page led me in. King sat on throne then turned to left like judge going back to cham-

bers. I didn't see his face. Queen started up
long narrow circular staircase & smiled at me
over shoulder. Then she had on metallic mask.
I said, "You are arrogant" & she answered, "It
is only a mirror of you."

K. was quite pleased with her first active
imagination trip, and I would have been, too.
She had held her own, been protected by her religion, mixed with glamorous people, and had
been confident enough to permit herself a humorous little acknowledgment of her own
shortcoming in the end. Whereas I had been
admitted to the throne room by a seedy janitor,
the king and queen were only young apathetic
actors, he was in a tar-covered box. The queen
said I could bring her a Coca-Cola, not diet, she
didn't have to diet; he asked for a knife to get out
of the box. I asked what I was to them. The king
said tiredly, "Express me." The girl playing queen
said: "You are nothing at all to me. I don't want
to be like you." When I asked them for their
blessing, he stuck out an oily constricted paw

from his black box. She, quick as a flash, performed an obscene gesture. On the way back, I had to pass through a corridor of derelict men while angry black fish mouthed at me through a glass. A young woman like the queen seemed to be in trouble, but when I attempted to risk helping her, a man slashed at me with a small sharp knife, nicking my left forearm.

The second low point in my week, high point in K.'s, was art therapy class. We were told to take whatever materials we chose and express ourselves however we liked. This time, K. couldn't wait to get started; in a previous class, in which we matched our art postcard choices with our personality types, K. had fallen in love with a "pugnacious, whimsical yellow and brown dotted leopard," as she described it in her notebook, from the Metropolitan Museum of Art. Since we were not allowed to keep our postcards, she had made a sketch of hers, and now was eagerly availing herself of paints, paste, and sparkles to render him in greater glory.

I, who had been drawing and painting all my life, suddenly found myself unable even to choose a medium. In my new role as sullen, sidekick daughter of a sparkling mother, I went up to the art therapist and said I couldn't seem to get started. She unrolled a long sheet of paper and had me lie down on it. Then she took a crayon and outlined my body and I think I colored that. Then she said why not take some paints and just swish colors around on pieces of paper, see what happens. By the end of the class, a long one, I had some wet sheets of pale colors, and K. had a spunky, sparkly, painted creature suitable for framing.

We didn't always go to the same classes. She had her rapid grief resolution workshops and I went to several days of Jungian perspectives and spiritual direction until I conceived a violent hatred for a priggish, self-important young man in one of the classes and decided to opt out. I went for walks around the lake and once I stole back to the art room and found that in the company of myself I could still draw and paint. I did a hanged man (with lots of sparkles) who was also dancing, and rendered from memory my favorite art postcard from the personality-type session: St. Francis meeting St. Dominic. At supper, I sat at the table with a Jesuit Jungian analyst who intimated that my attraction to this postcard could signal a reconciliation of opposites, which made me, in my present role, feel a bit better about myself.

By the fourth day, K. and I were wearying. She wrote in her notebook that the food was too rich and plentiful and her ankles were swelling and she was worried about me and my bad active imagination trip. I often wonder what it would have been like if we had suddenly looked at each other and said, "Hell, let's get out of here, and drive back to Asheville and cook some simple food and drink lots of wine and really do a number on all this journeying." But this had been my invitation, and we stuck it out. But we did withdraw unto ourselves more, and things got better.

One night, instead of dutifully writing in her journal about the day's workshops and lectures, K., from her bed, told me a story about the worst thing that had ever happened in her life—before she lost a son, that is. I was two at the time and don't remember the death of her father, but she and her mother left me with a friend in Asheville and they accompanied the casket on the train down to Birmingham, where he was to be buried. It was hot and the train stopped at all the stations so Southern Railway employees could pay their respects to my grandfather, who had been a much-loved railroad man.

"By the time we had the funeral in Birmingham, the . . . well . . . it was very hot and . . . oh, this is just terrible . . . the embalming fluid started leaking out of Daddy's mouth. I went up to the funeral director and instructed him to close the casket immediately. I couldn't tell mother why because she would have had to live with that image, and all the relatives were mad at me because they didn't get to see the body. I just had to live with it. I never told anyone until now."

Kathleen's kneeler for her son

On our last night at Kanuga, I dreamed that Mother and I were late to a church service at All Souls in Biltmore. There was a guest preacher in the middle of his sermon. He was like the self-important young man at the conference who had aroused my animosity. He was just at the end, just at his punch line, and our entrance interrupted him. Miffed, he called for a two-minute intermission. People started chatting and consulting their bulletins and he got furious and refused to finish. Then the rector, Neil Zabriskie, came up and went on with the service.

K. suggested we go for a walk before breakfast. She wanted to show me the St. Francis outdoor chapel she had discovered in one of her solo walks. I told her my dream and was somewhat vexed that she didn't want to dwell on it for long, she was so anxious to get to hers.

"I dreamed I was in All Souls, too. In the sacristy. I was waiting to go to communion, to the midweek noon service. I waited and waited. Finally, I thought it *must* be time to go into the church. But when I went in, it was empty and dark. All the lights were out. Nobody was there. I stayed awhile, all the same, waiting."

After breakfast there was a farewell ceremony. A young man danced around, selecting various conference members to be part of his magic circle to sum up the spirit of the conference. Neither K. nor I were chosen.

As we were packing in our room at the inn, a wasp flew out of a water glass and stung K. on the hand. We got ice from from the kitchen to put on it and I drove her car to Asheville. We made ourselves a light lunch, sat on the porch of K.'s condo, and talked. We had a small argument about whether there was time to visit a neighbor. We did, briefly. Then K. drove me to the airport for my 6:45 evening flight to Albany. I never saw her alive again.

Two weeks after her funeral at All Souls, I received a letter from Neil Zabriskie; here is the last part of it:

Jan. 17, 1990

. . . Marianne has been working on
Kathleen's kneeler. She says K. used an
amazing number of stitches—beautifully
done. It is a lovely piece. A bulletin re:
Kathleen: her spirit is still present at All
Souls. It seems at two mid-week Celebra-
tions of the Eucharist two or more
worshipers have heard the front door open &
Kathleen's unique footsteps coming up the
main aisle—& on both occasions, it occurred
at the usual time of her arrival, a few
minutes late. I have not been present, but it
apparently unnerved one man. A recently
confirmed Episcopalian, he didn't know
what he was getting in for in our church.

Trust things are going well with you.
You remain in my prayers.

Love,
Neil

"Her spirit is still present"

Evenings
at Five

A NOVEL AND FIVE STORIES

A Reader's Guide

Gail Godwin

A Conversation with Gail Godwin

ROB NEUFELD

Rob Neufeld is the book reviewer for the Asheville Citizen-Times *and director of the program "Together We Read" in North Carolina. At present, he is editing volume one of Gail Godwin's diaries.*

Rob Neufeld: In *Evenings at Five,* as Christina begins to commune with Rudy after his death, she imagines how other authors would write a ghost story about the experience. Then you write, "But this was Christina's story, and if she forced or finessed anything, she might miss the secret with her name on it." The spirit world is an easy sell for some, a hard sell for others. What are your thoughts about it?

Gail Godwin: My feelings about the spirit world are stronger than ever. I don't expect to see any ghosts of loved ones, but they do leave a vibrato.

There's the time when Christina gets a condolence letter from someone who says that loving someone after he has died is stronger because there's less interference. The static of what that person needs from you, what you need from him, isn't there. I wish I could write a ghost story. Very few satisfy me, and I know there's a possibility I could be satisfied.

RN: Many stories about women visited by ghosts are sad because the women can't overcome their grief and ultimately lose their preference for reality. Christina finds a different path. Is she a hero?

GG: She is—in that she keeps on living her life in the sense of the quest. The event has made her stronger through her knowledge about her love and her knowledge that she is lovable. I can't think of a novel that portrays a positive relationship with a ghost. Oh, I can think of one—*The Ghost and Mrs. Muir.* It's corny, but it qualifies for what a ghost story should be.

RN: What makes a good ghost story?

GG: It can't have any hokey hauntings or ap-
pearances. It has to grow out of the living person's history, perceptions, and needs. It can't be
inflicted on them. The ghost has to have lived
with them for a long time.

RN: How does the ghost manifest itself?

GG: It can go several ways. This leftover life
that refuses to die can inhabit the person and use
the living person as an instrument. It still doesn't
mean that an exterior thing has been planted in
them. It comes out of the living person's needs
and fears. In *The Ghost and Mrs. Muir,* Mrs. Muir
arrives at a house as a widow. A big temptation
for a widow is to lose her preference for reality.
What the attractive ghost does is get her back
into living life fully—smelling the sea. The sad-
dest thing in the story is when the ghost talks
about the relationship they could have had if he
had been alive. D. H. Lawrence has a story—

"The Borderline"—about a widow on a journey to meet her lover. Her dead husband ruins the whole thing. He's allowed to do so because she has incorporated certain powerful qualities of his. She grows increasingly powerful, and her new lover can't bear it.

RN: At the start of *Evenings at Five,* the reader finds himself dropped into a domestic scene already in progress. What is your relationship with readers? How do you lure them into your stories?

GG: This book didn't start off by my trying to lure any readers. I just wanted to sit there in my house every night around five o'clock, listen to all the sounds, and evoke the cocktail hour. After five pages, I had "tricked" myself into a new way of writing. It was a tempo, and I couldn't go wrong.

RN: This gets us to talking about music. You compare *Evenings at Five* to a sonata. Could you elaborate on that?

GG: A sonata has a certain form—a theme that's stated, then a companion theme. The two themes have a relationship. The sonata is resolved by moving or transforming into something that comes out of the materials, and yet is new. When Christina sits down in Rudy's chair and decides to drink a glass of red wine, she remembers how the priest had come to console her. She had asked him, "Where should I sit?" He said sit where you want, and she sits in Rudy's chair. Then, at the same time, she imagines herself on the sofa looking at Rudy. She imagines his personality and then she is able to be both herself and Rudy at once and then to be the life that was made by the two of them.

RN: Previous novels of yours involved religious thought. Are you trying to create a religion that not only works for you but also for the modern world?

GG: You said that I've been on a decades-long search for a powerful and centering spirit. I am. I go to church because it connects me with the beginning of my search at St. Mary's [Episcopal Church in Asheville]. Tom Miller, the priest at St. Gregory's in Woodstock, said, "We might as well learn to accept our inseparability from God." One contains a relationship between one-self and this Other—this powerful, centering spirit. I just live with it; there's no theorizing. There's just working at that relationship.

RN: In *Evenings at Five,* you say that Christina felt Rudy's presence more strongly once he was absent. One can then believe that with death, the sense of presence becomes everlasting. That's the kind of religious thought a scientific person can grasp. And then when the priest visits Christina, what does he say?

GG: He visits with a parishioner and he says the burial office: "Hope that is seen is not hope. Why hope for what is already seen?"

RN: Another good religious thought for a rationally minded person.

GG: There are some other good ones in *Evensong* [Godwin's previous novel].

RN: You know Paul Valéry's saying, "God made everything out of nothing. But the nothingness shows through." Do you agree with this?

GG: Something else shows through when you get to the bottom of nothingness. It's like a piece of black cheesecloth. There's a glow below it. This would make a good painting. You know, I find so much out about my characters by drawing them. [Some of Gail's artwork can be seen at www.gailgodwin.com.]

RN: At the end of "Old Lovegood Girls," Christina, having donated money to her alma mater, says, "I . . . like the idea of some girl like myself . . . knowing she may dream and study and play the innocent ingénue a little longer." Could you tell us a little more about being an ingénue?

GG: The ingénue is the girl who has all her options open. She's taken care of by others. There's time to play, to read and study, to learn things.

RN: Regarding your reflections on childhood, to what extent do you identify with the ingénue?

GG: I suddenly have the horrible feeling I've never been an ingénue. I had a dream when I was five or six—I was on a front lawn of a house and a mammy was bathing a blond-haired boy. I crept up to the boy and said, "Splash her." He does—and she comes crawling after me. I've always been an instigator. I've never been an ingénue. I don't think I was ever innocent. The first time I went to Sunday school, I came home and said I had pushed a little boy down the stairs. My mother called the church. She was told that no little boy had been pushed down the stairs.

RN: In what ways is it different applying your fiction writing to your own life rather than to invented characters? Are there special risks and special rewards?

GG: First, when I think I'm writing a memoir, I use fictional ploys and shapings, slipping in a fiction here and there. When I'm writing about other people, I'm writing about my internal cast of characters. In memoirs and in fiction, I will do anything to get to the quickening moment.

RN: The Christina stories are particularly candid and personal. In "Mother and Daughter Ghosts, A Memoir," you tell about your last time together with your mother before she died, when you felt threatened by her at a spirituality conference. You both had responded to an exercise by which you had to imagine yourselves meeting the king and queen of your psyches. In your mother's scenario, she was the heroine admired by the queen. In yours, you were snubbed by the queen.

GG: It's so funny and so horrible. I spent the last hours before my flight on my mother's porch, writing my criticisms of the conference, when I could have been spending precious time with her.

RN: That story stands as the only experience with your mother in the book, whereas in real life, you had many, including ones that celebrate the joy you both felt—well, the joy you share at the beginning of the "Mother and Daughter Ghosts" story. Do you sometimes make yourself laugh when you're writing?

GG: Something will happen in a scene, and I'll giggle. My humor surprises me. I don't plan it.

RN: In chapter 5 of *Evenings at Five,* after Christina returns home from the doctor following her scary blindness episode, she takes down Rudy's and her "brown-at-the-edges" cartoon of a woman saying to her snuggly mate, "I love these quiet evenings at home battling alcoholism." Next she disposes of all Rudy's medications, and recalls the party they attended shortly before his death

when Rudy, feeling time-pressured and exasper-
ated with small talk about cabbages and Brussels
sprouts, booms in his loud bass voice: "An outstanding cabbage would be a welcome addition to
this gathering." The humor is necessary to lighten
the pain, isn't it? If you go a distance in your story
without humor, do you sense that?

GG: Often during the course of remembering,
you bump back and forth between painful and
humorous material. Christina has been shaken by
her doctor's term *blotto,* and comforts herself with
Gil Mallow's recent remark that she and Rudy
made a "formidable" couple, a description she
prefers to "blotto." Thinking of the Mallows leads
her into the funny-awful memory of the dinner
party where they met. Whenever I read that dinner party passage aloud, people burst out laughing
and so do I. Yet at the time, Christina (and I!) suffered agonies and was furious. But now, with
Rudy gone, she misses the individual force of his
awful moment, and she has this great insight that
comforted me as I was writing the passage. I

quote from the book: "But now the absence of that force she could never quite modify or control has left an excavation in her life that cried out to be filled with his most awful moments."

RN: A nightmare has a powerful effect on Christina in *Evenings at Five*. Dreams populate your fiction and daydreams constantly mix in. Might we consider you an advocate of the dream world?

GG: Jungian analysis is an ongoing graduate course for me about the one-third of my life when I'm asleep. I could index the figures, settings, and cross-references. My dreams are definitely a commentary on what my unconscious is trying to tell me—what's being neglected and what's being falsified.

RN: Do bad guys have bad dreams?

GG: Your dreams point to things you need to pay attention to: "Hey, Macbeth, that forest is moving toward your castle."

RN: In your preface, you say you envisioned stories that would pounce on "those places in Christina's journey that mark a turning point for her." Two stories portray experiences that preceded the deaths of your parents; and two other stories, those of your priest and of Robert. How central a concern is it to you to come up with an answer to death?

GG: I'm not trying to come up with an answer to death. I'm trying to engage with death. Death is not an enemy at all; it's a room I haven't been allowed into yet. The barriers may open into unexpected landscapes.

RN: Do you plan on adding Christina stories to future editions of *Evenings at Five*?

GG: This is by no means a finished product. I have other Christina stories. Eventually, *Evenings at Five* will stand by itself again. When my editor had called me to say that *Evenings at Five* would be coming out in paperback and would look thin, she asked, "Do you have anything else?" I sent her the Christina stories I had. When I add new Christina stories, the whole new book will be called *The Passion of Christina* and will have stories that go from childhood to old age—about twenty-five stories.

*Reading Group Questions
and Topics for Discussion*

1.   Let's start with the very first sentence in *Evenings at Five:* "Five o'clock sharp." Do you hear a bell tolling? What does this one sentence tell you about what you're about to read? The phrase is repeated on page 29. How do you react to hearing it again? Five o'clock is associated with a ritual in Christina's house. A ritual—originally meaning a prescribed religious ceremony—has taken on the meaning of a regular household activity. Is there such a thing as a household religion—and if so, what composes it?

2.   Are stronger memories associated with rituals than with other events? What kinds of experiences make the strongest memories? What kinds of sensations and associations does Godwin latch on to as Christina evokes the cocktail hour?

3. Are rituals necessary in helping us avoid feeling vulnerable in lives easily dominated by our own weaknesses? How does Christina use rituals to counter her ritual alcohol drinking?

4. Some memories are "graven on the heart" (page 16) and others strike familiar chords. Chapter 1 ends with Rudy answering Christina's question, "What are you thinking?" by telling her, "I wasn't thinking. I was hearing music." Does Christina attain this kind of sensitivity in a way? Is what she hears on page 17 a kind of music? To a certain way of hearing, is everything music, including Rudy's answering machine message (pages 38–39), to which Christina applies the Gregorian term *melisma* (an ornamental phrasing of a word or syllable)? The last chapter, "Coda," reminds us that Godwin has composed a sonata in *Evenings at Five*. In what ways can you sense or hear a sonata in the novel?

5. Godwin says that, after writing the first five pages of *Evenings,* she had tricked herself into a

Evenings at Five, to witness the growth of a major work. How do the five stories connect to *Evenings*? What major themes are developing? Where are the gaps? What additional stories would you like to see?

17. At the end of "Possible Sins," Father Weir suggests using a favorite food as a password for spiritual communication rather than a memorable piece of wisdom. What information do you use for private passwords in e-mail accounts or as personal information to confirm your identity with credit-card companies? What really sticks in your mind?

18. What fairy tale does "Largesse" evoke? Do modern women have to create a body of stories to counter the messages of traditional fairy tales?

19. Both "Largesse" and "Old Lovegood Girls" involve fellow airplane passengers who play roles in ushering Christina into her story. Are each of the Christina stories a mythological

journey? If so, what insight or dividend does Christina retrieve from each descent?

20. How does Godwin struggle with the idea of the ingénue? In her interview, she says that she had never been an ingénue. Yet in "Old Lovegood Girls," she acknowledges an attraction to the old Southern way of life and the importance of such a concept to her father. At the heart of this issue are Christina's views on goodness, expressed in her essay for Miss Petrie. Does Christina's belief in goodness, even though it's a revision of the traditional model, indicate an attachment to the old ideal? Or does Christina reject the ideal as a product of the "market for brides"? How do you think Godwin views marriage?

21. In "Waltzing with the Black Crayon," Kurt Vonnegut issues some rules for writing. Do you agree with them? Do you have a list of rules?

22. In what ways is "Mother and Daughter Ghosts, A Memoir" a ghost story? Why does the term *ghost* apply to the daughter as well as the mother?

23. What is it that causes Godwin to slip into the role that attaches to her at the conference in "Mother and Daughter"? Does every situation contain a dynamic that has prescribed roles, each of which someone has to fill? Was Godwin looking for a way out of what had been developing at the conference? What might have been and what were her ways out?

24. What do Godwin's and her mother's imagination exercises say about them at the moment they compose them?

25. "Mother and Daughter" contains a powerful revelation—the mother's admission of what she had witnessed and redressed at her father's funeral. It comes under the heading "the

worst thing that had ever happened in her life." What function does revelation play in Godwin's fiction? What kinds of questions elicit revelations? "What is the worst thing?" is one. Another kind of revelation leads off "Waltzing with the Black Crayon." What are the different kinds of revelation?

PHOTOGRAPH BY ERIC RASMUSSEN.

ABOUT THE AUTHOR

GAIL GODWIN is the three-time National Book Award nominee and bestselling author of eleven critically acclaimed novels, including *A Mother and Two Daughters*, *Violet Clay*, *Father Melancholy's Daughter*, and *Evensong*. She has received a Guggenheim Fellowship, a National Endowment for the Arts grant for both fiction and libretto writing, and the Award in Literature from the American Academy and Institute of Arts and Letters. She has written libretti for ten musical works with the composer Robert Starer. Currently she is writing her twelfth novel, *Queen of the Underworld*.

Visit her Web site at www.gailgodwin.com.

THE FINISHING SCHOOL

A Novel

by GAIL GODWIN

Justin Stokes would never forget the summer she turned fourteen, nor the woman who transformed her bleak adolescent life into a wondrous place of brilliant color. In the little pondside hut also known as the "finishing school," eccentric, free-spirited Ursula DeVane opened up a world full of magical possibilities for Justin, teaching her valuable lessons of love and loyalty, and encouraging her to change, to learn, to grow. But the lessons of the finishing school have their dark side as well, as Justin learns how deep friendship can be shattered by shocking, unforgivable betrayal.

Published by Ballantine Books
Available wherever books are sold